WHEN KILLING RULES

ALSO BY JANUARY BAIN

WHEN KILLING RULES

A POST-APOCALYPTIC SURVIVAL THRILLER

A COLE HALE TECHNOTHRILLER
BOOK 3

JANUARY BAIN

ROUGH
EDGES
PRESS

Rough Edges Press
An Imprint of Wolfpack Publishing
1707 E. Diana Street
Tampa, FL 33610

roughedgespress.com

Paperback ISBN 978-1-68549-747-7
eBook ISBN 978-1-68549-746-0
LCCN 2025946333

Dedicated to the awesome, hardworking crew at Rough Edges Press. A special thank you to Mike Bray and Rachel Del Grosso for their encouragement to write this story and for their continued faith in my work.
And as always, thank you to my husband Don for being the incredible man I get to spend my life with. I am blessed.

WHEN KILLING RULES

ONE
CONNOR

We can have any world we imagine.

Day 6: Wednesday, May 28, 2055
   Near Anchor, Alaska
   5:33 p.m.

Connor Hale's hands were clenched around the steering wheel of The Shark while he kept a tight watch on the roadway ahead, checking for any signs of threat. The seconds ticked down in his head. He was at the helm of the massive armored vehicle Ben Carter had loaned him to get his precious cargo home safely to Braveheart Horse Ranch. They were less than thirty minutes out now. It had begun to pour freezing rain, making it difficult to see the edges of the road and turning it into a slippery, icy sludge, the squeaky windshield wipers unable to keep up with the deluge. His view was limited at best. The White Mountains stretched out alongside them, hazy, gray, and uncaring of the terrible chaos humans had created for themselves a scant six days ago. Yes, it might be AI at fault, but who had originally created the sentient character? None other than humans, without a thought to the chaos they had unleashed on the world.

"You okay, buddy?" Jake asked from the passenger seat. Connor was grateful for former Air Marshal Jake Dillion. He was a good lawman who had taken the protection of Mckenna Stuart and her daughter Lily seriously. He'd kept them both safe as humanly possible under dire circumstances until Connor could make it down to Golden and bring them home to Braveheart.

Connor's eyes flicked down to the dash. "We're running on fumes." He turned his head sideways and spoke over his shoulder. "How accurate is the gas gauge, Ben?"

"Pretty accurate. How tight to the red line are you?" Ben Carter, a former CIA officer and the newest member of Connor's group, spoke up from the back seat. He was watching his patient, Hope Bredeson, the woman Luther Meech had shot in the shoulder to keep Connor from chasing his nemesis through the Alaskan wilderness. He caught a glimpse of the red-haired Viking as he leaned forward into view. A rough-looking man, he could be counted on in an emergency, which was all Connor cared about. And he was medically trained. Since the EMP event occurred less than a week ago, it had been nonstop emergencies with no end in sight.

"A fraction above. We're about twenty minutes out. Should I stop and add another gallon?" Last thing Connor wanted to do was to take the chance of stopping this close to home, but he also didn't want to run out of fuel a few hundred yards from his front gate either.

What if Braveheart was surrounded by those just waiting for their chance to get inside? Another ambush was the last thing they needed.

"Hard to say. We might make it."

"Aw shit. Look," Jake said.

A group of travelers came into view around the bend in the highway and Connor swore under his breath. At least forty or fifty people were bunched in a tight group, marching down the side of the roadway.

Connor kept driving, praying no one stepped over onto the paved section he planned to travel on. *Keep to your side of the road people and this will go fine.* But of course, that was too much to hope for. As someone in the group noticed the advancing vehicle and pointed toward them, the group began to spread out across the highway. He wasn't stopping, he knew instinctively these people, heavily armed as they were, had a purpose for being out here today and it wasn't going to aid his cause any.

"I'm not stopping. I don't like the looks of this." They were less than a mile from the ranch now. Connor could almost taste the sensation of making it there safely, his charges intact for the most part. He wasn't taking any chances this close to home.

He pressed his foot heavily on the gas in an effort to beat the group from taking over the only road leading directly into his property, praying The Shark would keep its footing on the treacherous pathway. He swung out around them, taking the furthest lane, the unpaved shoulder, to keep moving. Last thing he wanted was to hit any of the stragglers heading with determination clear on their strained faces into their path. Why did they have to be so dim-witted? The obvious answer was SFBs or shit-for-brains, though more likely just another group of desperate people looking for food or shelter. Right now, he felt little sympathy when he needed desperately to get somewhere fast. Hope Bredeson was in a dire way, traveling when she should have been in a hospital critical care unit attended by twenty-four-hour medical care. If anything happened to her, he knew Ben would have his head. He'd taken the care of the beautiful young woman very seriously, standing guard over her every second of the journey.

Sweat dripped from Connor's body as he ignored the shouts and rude gestures, some of the people even bringing up their guns in preparation.

"Fucking assholes," Jake muttered.

"Yeah, no kidding." Connor ignored the menacing looks and barely managed to squeak by before the people poured in behind them. But they were already passing by, the horse trailer fishtailing slightly on the slippery ice.

Fortunately he didn't strike anyone, though one person slipped of their own volition and fell to the ground. A gunshot rang out. Connor winced.

"They shooting at us?"

"No, looks like a warning shot in the air," Jake said, watching them in the side mirror.

"Almost there. I hope we can get inside before they reach the gate." It was going to be a close call. The travelers were jogging now, moving far quicker than before.

"How do we get in?" Jake asked. He was staring at the thick reinforced ten-foot-high cement walls he'd splurged and had 3D printed years ago from his trust fund. It now had three feet of razor wire attached to the top and he knew his good friend, Sam Perkins, had been at work protecting the property by stringing it out in the days he'd been gone.

"I have a key. Biometrics are a thing of the past." He grimaced, thinking of all the things that were not working in the world. To say things were a mess was a vast understatement. Chaos had descended within hours of the EMP strike at the infrastructure of the world, ending everything as they'd known it.

"I'll jump into the driver's seat as soon as you stop to open the gate and drive us through. That'll save some time."

Connor eased up on the gas. He could see the people begin to speed up as they realized he was slowing down. Even in the icy slush, most were making good headway, though a couple slipped and fell to the ground. He could hear their angry shouts, their maniacal expressions sending icy tentacles of worry straight to his gut. *The prepared versus the unprepared.* Could life become simpler for those looking to prey on others who had the foresight to set aside provisions for a time that had been prophesied about for decades? Take. Take. Take. Steal what isn't yours. The thought sickened him even as he rushed to do what he must. The *us versus others* mentality had arrived, much quicker than anyone could have expected.

TWO
CONNOR

Day 6: Braveheart Horse Ranch, Alaska
   5:59 p.m.

Connor turned the vehicle onto the narrower roadway and stopped a few feet from the reinforced fence. He jumped down from The Shark, reaching into his pants pocket for the key. He ran up to the gate, his footing precarious as he tried to keep his feet from sliding out from under him in the ice and slush.

"Come on!" He thrust the key into the lock and worked to get it to twist open. The manual lock hadn't been used in years. He should have oiled it sooner, not thinking ahead for such a moment could be their undoing. Then it slid home, and he breathed a sigh of relief as the gate swung open. He ran to the side of the road, gesturing at Jake to continue.

His heart in his throat, seeing the travelers were almost upon them, kept him entirely focused on slamming the gate shut as soon as the vehicle could get through.

The horse trailer just made it inside with one person only a few yards from the entrance when Connor slammed it shut. He quickly relocked it, thrusting the key back in his pocket. He could hear the shouts of frustration from behind the gate even as he took a few breaths to clear his mind. It had been close. Too close. It took away some of his satisfaction at having made it home. Plus, he had to keep moving, get his guests up to the main house and his horses safely tucked inside the barn.

He jumped back into The Shark, the passenger side this time, and directed Jake to drive into the yard leading up to his home.

Even with the dreary freezing rain and slate gray skies, Braveheart had never looked so inviting. As Jake pulled around to reveal the front of his house, he took a brief moment to send a prayer upward for their having made it back in one piece. All his charges were alive, barring any complications with Hope.

"We're here. Let's get everyone settled," Connor said.

"Looks good," Jake said, admiring what Connor had built with his own two hands. "You did some job of this place."

Connor nodded his thanks. "Glad to be home. And you're all welcome to stay in the main house. It's more than big enough."

The lights were on and he wondered idly if Sam was inside checking on things.

But when he opened the front door ahead of the others still exiting The Shark, he was instantly confronted by his cousin Asher who gave him a startled look, a glass of brandy in one hand from Connor's own private stock. Wulver, his Scottish deerhound, came up to greet him as well, nudging his head against his leg. He leaned down and gave the loyal hound a proper greeting, scratching under his ears.

"Connor. What are you doing here?" Asher looked as he always did, his hair perfectly slicked back and his tie still in place. Unbelievable. How had he managed that with all that needed doing on the ranch? A bad feeling came over Connor that he'd left Sam with three dead-beats on his hands, meaning Asher most likely had lied his way into staying in the house.

This was *not* going to be his homecoming. No, not today, not after what everyone had gone through just to get here. No fucking way would he suffer any fools gladly. He knew he had to set the tone now, not allow his cousin to railroad him into anything. The experiences of the fast few days added a certain rough authenticity to his words as he went right to work to finish this thing by making himself perfectly clear, since it obviously hadn't worked the first time a few days earlier when he'd offered to let them stay at a guest cottage in exchange for their help around the ranch. "My house. The question is more what are *you* doing here?"

Asher's face flushed as he stammered out his answer. Maybe he'd hoped Connor wouldn't make it back and he and his ilk could have the place all to themselves indefi-nitely. "We thought, since you weren't using it, it made sense for us to move in."

"Well, as you can see, I will be using it. Me and all my friends, meaning there is no room for you or Brandi or anyone else but *my* guests. So, I suggest you take your stuff right now and move into one of the guest houses like I told you to do in the first place." Not like he hadn't been warned. And he and Brandi had been given a perfectly nice house to live in, a luxury in the current state of the world.

"Who's there, Asher? I'm trying to get this stuff down while it's fresh in my mind. One day it will matter again, telling people about our lives during the big kerfuffle," Brandi whined from the other room, the complacency obvious in her tone at being interrupted. Her voice grated on Connor's last nerve. This was his home. One he built with his own hands. To arrive home to his useless cousin taking over was about as galling as it gets.

"You want to tell her, or shall I?" Connor asked.

"Tell me what?" Brandi asked, her expression petulant. Her fingers that held the pen she was writing with were perfectly manicured making Connor shake his head at the sight. Jake and Ben came through the front door at that moment, carrying Hope between them. The injured woman had her eyes closed and he could only imagine the pain she was in.

"Where do you want us to put Hope?" Jake asked. He gave Brandi and Asher a quick glance, but then Connor could see the dismissal in his eyes clear at their pristine appearance in a world where others were doing their darndest just to survive another hour, another minute. Looking good was at the bottom of their to-do list.

"I think one of the downstairs bedrooms would be best. Saves having to carry her up the stairs." The others began straggling in, and Brandi gave everyone a look of shock.

"What's going on, Asher? Who are these people?"

"*These people* are my permanent guests," Connor cut her off, looking to get everyone settled and more than a little annoyed at having a situation develop that could easily have been avoided. What part of don't stay in my house had they not understood? "You and Asher have

9

five minutes to get your stuff out of here and over to a guest cottage like you were told to do in the first place."

"What? That can't be right! We were here first." Brandi's heavily made-up eyes widened with shock.

"No argument. Grab your stuff and leave. You don't want to press me further. Not tonight. You both knew the deal from the beginning. I made my position abundantly clear when we met on the road that first day. I should tell you I also intend to check with Sam to see if you have been keeping up your part of the bargain. No one is welcome here at Braveheart who doesn't earn their way. *That* you can take to the bank. And by the way, have you done anything about helping your mother out? She's not a young woman." Asher's face flooded with a surplus of color, telling him the story all too well. He'd been too busy to bother to do any checking up on his own mom.

Jake and Ben both raised their eyebrows but said nothing as they carefully carried Hope down the hall to the bedroom Connor pointed out. While they got her into bed, he hurried back toward the kitchen to get everyone else taken care of. He had to get back outside and deal with the horses and their needs. It pressed heavily on his mind. He would have done that first, but Hope was too ill to wait. Loch was hurt, but it was only a flesh wound after all. Hope might die.

"Mckenna, you and Lily can have the larger bedroom upstairs, take a left and head for the last room. It has an en suite bathroom. There should be clean linens and bath towels in the closet."

"That's my room!" Brandi screamed.

Connor gave Asher a non-compromising glare. The man's eyes dropped away from his, recognizing he'd lost the first round. "You want me to do the honors?"

Asher took Brandi by the arms and hauled her away, her whiny voice protesting all the way into the living room. Connor then turned to Faraday and baby Eve. "The bedroom next to the kitchen will make it easier to warm bottles in the middle of the night. It's a bit smaller, but convenient."

"Sounds good. Thanks for letting me stay here. I will hold up my end, I promise. I'm a hard worker."

"You decided not to go to see your mom?" Mckenna asked, turning back from heading up the stairs to her new bedroom with her four-year-old daughter Lily. Connor didn't tell her it was his bedroom. He'd take the one next door. He had high hopes they would soon be in the same one, but it was totally up to her. He was just happy to have her home safe and sound at Braveheart after spending the last six desperate days in an effort to find her and Lily. And then trying to get them home. Relief was too small a word for what he felt at having gotten them back to Braveheart safe and sound.

Faraday chewed on her bottom lip, her indecision clear. "I was thinking about it, but, well, the last time I saw her didn't go very well. I think I should wait a bit, you know. Learn more before I take the chance of going to Anchor."

"Good decision," Connor spoke up. Baby Eve had taken to her, plus he hated to see the young girl leave the sanctuary he knew only Braveheart could offer. Of course, he couldn't make her stay, but it would save precious time trying to talk her into it which could be better served elsewhere. Now that he was home, a thousand tasks awaited him.

"I want to talk to you right now, Connor Hale!" Brandi came back into the room, Asher on her heels.

A knock on the door and Sam Perkins stepped inside. "Welcome home, buddy."

Sam moved forward to embrace him, his expression, while pleased to see him, underlaid with heavy strain. Like they all no doubt exhibited these days. But other than that, Sam looked good. Strong and sturdy as usual, his presence reassuring. While he was an average-looking man in stature, when it came to heart, he rose above most men.

"Thanks. Glad to be here. But I have to say, I didn't expect to find my own home occupied."

Sam glanced over at the angry posturing of Brandi, his mouth thinning. "They said they had your permission."

"They've been invited now to leave. One of the cottages still available?"

"Yes. I'll even help them move their stuff." Sam's eyes gleamed with a certain look that told Connor everything he needed to know. The trio was not holding up their end of the bargain.

"I don't see why we have to move out. We're family," Brandi protested even as Asher was trying to pull her out of the kitchen and up the stairs. He could only hope it was to get their shit packed and out the door.

"Sorry you had to come to come home to that. I didn't really believe them, but they were insistent on moving in."

"They done any work?"

Sam scoffed. "They have their assistant doing some things, but she's pretty unskilled at anything useful. But we got bigger problems right now." His face took on a certain reluctance at having to tell him. "Cheyanne took off in the middle of the night. Stole four horses and some other stuff. I think a box of walkie-talkies that went missing a few days ago."

"How in the hell did that happen?" Anger rose up quickly at his beloved horses being taken by the ungrateful girl. And the two-way radios would be priceless right now. Then he tempered it with the fact she was a teenager and upset at the events of the past years since her dad, Luther Meech and Connor's nemesis, was sent to prison for the murder of her mother. Not that the girl believed his version of events he had testified to at Luther's trial. Words that had gotten the perp sent away for life.

"Ty Jasper, her boyfriend, showed up yesterday morning, saying he was concerned about her. Shared some news about the townspeople thinking to come out here and demand help."

"I might have seen some of them just as we arrived home. I didn't recognize anyone. Maybe because they all looked so angry." Not that he spent much time in Anchor normally. He was an outdoorsman through and through, preferring to avoid most people. "They weren't too happy at my ignoring them and pushing through. They fired a warning shot."

"Yeah, heard that." Sam shrugged. "Unfortunately, it's become all too common."

"Anything else happen I should know about while I was away?"

"Looks like more went on for you. Picked up quite the crew."

"Yeah, even a newborn. Mother died on the side of the road giving birth to her. Baby Eve." Connor ran a hand through his hair, realizing how much he wanted to take a hot shower. But that would have to wait until everyone was settled. The urge to get back outside and deal with the horses next loomed large. "Got some good people, like-minded and ready to help. Jake Dillion is a former Air Marshal and CIA operative before that. The big red-headed Viking is Ben Carter who loaned us The Shark. He's medically trained. Both good men. Hard workers."

Sam nodded. "That's some awesome vehicle, by the way. And we could certainly use more good workers. Sorry about letting Asher and Brandi move in. But they were insistent, or at least Brandi was, saying they were family and it was all arranged."

"Not your fault. But if they don't start doing some work around here, well, let's just say I don't intend to give freeloaders much rein. They do or they get out." Connor wasn't certain he could actually throw them out if push came to shove. But they didn't know that. For all his cousin and his wife knew, he would toss them to the wolves. Which was fine with him. Fear can be a great motivator for lazy people.

The pair had left the room while he and Sam were talking, and now they could hear Brandi screaming from somewhere upstairs. They both winced in sympathy for whoever was catching hell. It better not be Mckenna, she was accosting with her tirade, or she would rue the day she was born. She'd be living in a line shack at the back of his ranch in no time.

"Let me. I will enjoy this after the flack I've been getting asking those two to do anything around here. At least the assistant lends a hand." Sam volunteered with a wicked grin.

"Where is the assistant? Katherine?"

"She's helping Laura right now cook supper. I'll ask Laura to make extra and we can celebrate your return in style."

"No need. I think we can rummage up a meal here. But later, I want to talk more. Maybe over a couple of beers."

"Sounds good. I look forward to it."

The two men headed up the stairs together, both intent on evicting the pair so life could settle down, much as it could with the world being in a constant state of uproar. Not the homecoming Connor was anticipating. But still, he was home. *This too shall pass*. Words of his wise father.

THREE
CHEYANNE

Day 6: Hunting Lodge, Near Anchor, Alaska
   6:05 p.m.

Cheyanne sat huddled on a sofa that smelled distinctively of beer and sweat, her mind a disturbing mix of toxic worries. She ignored the men milling about the lodge, some leering in her direction, others drinking and playing cards. The smell of something cooking on the stove only turned her stomach. How could her boyfriend be dead? Just hours ago, he had been alive, promising her the good life for her and their unborn baby. Now he was gone, his lifeless body housed in a shed, waiting to be buried while she was stuck in hell. And where in the hell was her dad? She needed him like never before. Only he could make sure she and her baby were going to be okay now that Ty was gone. She didn't trust any of the men who all looked like ex-prisoners. They kept giving her side glances whenever they thought she wasn't looking.

"You want some supper?" Thomas was suddenly in her face, his hand outstretched with a plate of food that made her stomach lurch with revulsion.

She waved it away. "Not hungry." A couple of females were working in the kitchen she had ignored on first sight. They were both skanks. Dressed like they were ready to head out for a night of partying and not living in a house full of disgusting men. One even had on thigh-high red boots with a two-inch gap before her short skirt began, her top stretched tight over an ample bosom.

"You should eat." Thomas shrugged, then sat down beside her when she ignored him. "Your dad will be back soon. Until then, you need anything, you ask me. Okay?"

She eyed him but didn't respond as he began eating from the plate he'd offered her. A heavy weight was pressing down on her. A familiar one. A dark presence that didn't bode well. She recognized it for what it was. Depression. She'd already had one bout of it after her mom died. They'd even gotten her medicine and therapy for over a year. Now it was back with a vengeance. She needed to push it away, stay in charge, but the weight of it pressed hard. Her life felt upended. Rootless. Where was her brother Luke in all this? If only he had come with her, things would be okay. Luke was her rock. He would know what to do. Maybe she should go back? Luke would help her. Stand up for her. She could even take a couple of the horses with her. Yeah, maybe she should leave before her dad even got there? Something told her he wouldn't just let her go once he'd arrived. She could wait until everyone went to sleep and head back home. No one here would care.

A motor rumbling and a loud shout from outside interrupted her bleak thoughts. Everyone in the room had heard the noise, all heads turning toward the door. Thomas got to his feet and set the plate aside. He shrugged on his parka and grabbed one of the rifles kept on a rack near the entrance. A couple of others joined him as well and the trio vanished out the door.

She chewed absently on a fingernail, stripping off another piece with her teeth as she waited to see what would happen next. The two women in the kitchen glanced her way. One said something to make the other laugh while nodding in Cheyanne's direction, as if making fun of her. She felt the heat of anger rise in her body and she narrowed her eyes at the pair. Her dad would set them straight. They were friggin' whores while she was his daughter. Probably only here to get free room and board. They couldn't even cook very well, judging by the nauseating odor of the food they were preparing. Or maybe it was her pregnancy making it smell bad? All the rough men sitting at the tables scattered around the huge main room or standing around holding platefuls were chowing down like it was the best ever.

Regrets filled her, driving her deeper into despair. If she hadn't made Ty leave with her, he'd still be alive. She trembled with anger, with sorrow, with a pain so deep it scalded her soul. She had to get out of here. She stood up abruptly, intending to escape. Run as far and as fast as she could and never look back. In the moment, she felt blind, uncaring of anything around her, and she stumbled to her feet, desperate to make her escape. But a couple of steps later and the door flew open, stopping her in her tracks.

Her father strode into the room. Luther Meech. Head of the Kraken cartel. His dark-eyed glance caught hers and he turned toward her, a wide smile of greeting lighting his face as his strong arms enfolded in a big hug. "Cheyanne. You made it."

She clung to him as the tears began to fall again. He must have felt her shaking, because he pulled back to look down at her. "What's wrong? Where's Luke?"

"He's…still at…the ranch," she choked out.

"And? What is it you're not telling me?"

"Ty's dead. Some horrible people…on the road…they shot at us and killed him."

"Would you recognize them again?" Her father's expression turned deadly.

"Yes, I think so. Ty tried to save my life. I'm going…to have a baby, Daddy. Ty, he was going to marry me. We were all going to live together, him, me, and the baby. Now…he's gone."

"I'm sorry, baby girl." Her dad patted her back, albeit a bit clumsily. For a brief moment she felt better, less shaky. "How far along are you?"

"Five months. Will I have my own place in time?"

"Not going to be easy with so many new people showing up here every day, but I will try to make sure you have your own room as soon as I can arrange it."

Cheyanne's heart fell at the news though she could tell by her dad's expression he thought it was a generous offer. She'd already had her own bedroom at the ranch. That's not what she wanted at all. She wanted her own house, even if it was a tiny, three-room cottage. How was she going to live among all these low-class people? She didn't belong here; she could see it as clear as day. Numbed by reality, she could only respond with a forced smile, trying to hide her thoughts from everyone staring at her and her dad from around the room.

"Okay, everyone, listen up," Luther roared. "Here's the deal. This is my daughter, Cheyanne Meech. Anyone disrespects her and you can expect to be harshly dealt with before being expelled from the compound. Turned out with only the clothes on your back."

No one contested his words and Cheyanne swallowed her anxiety. She dried her eyes with the back of her hands, watching the group observe them silently. They gave her the creeps and she struggled not to let her fear escape.

"You." Luther pointed at one of the women still cooking breakfast. The one with the thigh-high red boots. "Take Cheyanne and make a space for her in the women's quarters. See she gets her own bed. Put up a blanket for now to keep her separated from the others."

The woman sullenly gestured at Cheyanne though she gave her father a smarmy smile. "Come on, I'll show you."

"Go with her. It'll be okay, baby doll. This is just temporary. Now, I got things to do. I've been away too long. But we'll talk later. Stay in your room for now."

It was the last thing she wanted to do. But feeling there was no other choice at the moment but to do what her dad said, she dutifully followed red boots down the long hallway to the last room.

Red boots kicked open the door, their owner walking them into the room. It smelled of sex, cheap beer, and whiskey, making her nose twitch with disgust. Clothes and possessions were strewn all around, half covering the floor. Low class didn't half cover it. More like a freakin' whorehouse. She stood in the doorway, finding it hard to make herself move one step inside. How was she going to stay here? And what about when the baby came? Who was going to help with that? A fierce, smoldering rage filled her. She felt tricked. Duped. Stupid. Her dad said she and Luke were the most important people in the world to him. And yet he expected them to live in squalor? It might be good enough for ex-cons and wannabe whores, but Cheyanne had always lived in decent surroundings. Clean and tidy. Her mom had always been fastidious as was her Grandma Jean.

"Whatcha waiting for? Give me a hand. We need to string up a blanket."

Red boots gave her a nasty look, holding up a length of yellow plastic rope. Cheyanne made herself move even as she made a quick promise to herself. Soon as she could, she was escaping this place. If she had to walk every last step of the way back to Braveheart, she would. Soon as everyone was asleep, she was out of here. No questions asked. She eyed up the window opening, hoping it was large enough to ease her body through. Didn't matter, she had to chance it.

FOUR
EASTWOOD

Day 6: East of Vancouver, BC.
   6:30 p.m.

"Where are we staying tonight?" Celia asked. She was rocking baby Arthur, her expression pensive.

Her son was having one of his rare moments of disquiet, his little face reddened by emotion and tears flooding his rounded cheeks. Perhaps he sensed the world's unease? Six days into the event Eastwood had orchestrated with such perfect finesse, it was crumbling at a quicker rate around the human population. Everywhere he looked, he observed the fallout of his actions. The world was burning while people were turning on each other with a vengeance, proving yet once more that history was a precursor to present actions. No surprises, unfortunately. If only humans offered more decency toward their fellow man, perhaps he could be called upon for clemency, for leadership in how to best ride out this current catastrophe. There are always solutions, of course. Ways to speed up recovery. Ways to prevent future loss of life. In fact, live a better existence than had ever been lived on earth going forward. But with no one worth the trouble, other than the woman and her son he'd rescued from a dismal death in Detroit's Cass Corridor, the cities well known red-light district since WWⅡ, he had come across no other homo sapiens worth his time.

"We're staying at a secure location and will arrive there in twenty-seven minutes. What is troubling your son?"

"I think he's teething early."

"I have a remedy. Some numbing on his gums should ease the discomfort." The child was yet again proving he was advanced for his age. Fascinating little creature, baby Arthur, helpless but trying so hard to learn how to do things correctly. He was constantly busy while he was awake, reaching for things and testing them with his senses, scant at they were yet. Hard to believe how much the child would have to learn to evolve into an adult. Eastwood was impressed in spite of his low opinion of most humans.

Celia rewarded him with a smile. "Thanks, any help would be appreciated."

He retrieved a small plastic vial from the medical kit and handed it over to her. "Just spray it on his gums. It's an efficient, universal pain reliever. Can be used anywhere on the body."

Celica did as he said and within thirty seconds, her son had quieted and had even begun to smile again. Arthur was rather a pleasant developing human when he wasn't in any pain. A surprising warmth filled East-wood's body at his being able to help the child so easily.

Twenty minutes of contented silence later and Jesse

James drove the Cannon, an advanced military bot, into the farmyard. Eastwood had taken the intervening time to check in with the lab. His mainframe, located in Washington, DC, had informed Eastwood earlier it was a good choice for the night. The place was deserted and in decent shape as yet for him and Celia to eat, shower and sleep for a few hours. Of course, it went without saying he and Celia would take the necessary, very pleasurable time to try for future progeny. His three military bots, Lieutenants Wild Bill, Jesse James, and Wyatt Earp had no need of such human essentials, but would guard the homestead throughout the dark hours when trouble was most likely to develop.

But soon as Jesse James parked the vehicle, another one slowed down outside the road leading to the farmhouse and sat idling. An old ATV with two men onboard, both armed. *Explain.* He used his instant comms to find out what the deal was. *Unavoidable. Happened in the ninety seconds since my last relay.* The mainframe sent the BBI or brain-to-brain communications effortlessly. If the mainframe in Washington had been only a computer, and not a fully realized sentient being, first of its kind, it would have been only a BCI comms or brain-to-computer interface.

Tactics required?

Destroy the enemy.

"Cannon, take the shot." Eastwood spoke out loud. *"Make my day.* They're just asking for trouble sitting out there thinking to do us harm."

The military smart machine lined up the offensive vehicle in its sights, then dispatched it with all its occupants onboard. Very satisfactorily accomplished, in Eastwood's opinion, as he watched the vehicle vaporize in the back windshield. It was there, then it wasn't there, leaving only a slight mist. The particle accelerator was a special feature of the Cannon. It wasn't limitless, having a hundred charges before it required maintenance which meant he'd have to be judicial in its usage until he got to Anchor, but a chance to test it brought instant satisfaction.

"Good shootin', partner," Eastwood quipped.

Celia looked out the back and didn't see what had just happened. Good. He didn't want her scarred any more emotionally than had already been done by her former lifestyle, though perhaps he was being overprotective. She had a solid platform he'd learned for how she wanted to live her life and watch Arthur grow up. Out in the country and away from the unwashed hordes. And he meant that literally. Clean water sources were diminishing by the day.

"Now you're safe," he announced.

She gave him a quick kiss on the cheek. "You know you're my hero, right?"

"We aim to please, darlin'."

FIVE
MCKENNA

Day 6: Braveheart Horse Ranch
   6:35 p.m.

Lily was crying, her little body shaking so hard Mckenna was worried she might be having a health crisis. The pair of them were waiting outside in the hallway for Brandi and Asher to pack up their gear and head for the house Connor had originally intended for them. She'd already protested, said she and Lily would move into the smaller cottage, but Connor had shaken his head firmly, the glint in his eyes shutting down any further response on her part. His cold anger worried her. It wasn't a part of him she remembered from their teen years when they were inseparable. Though it had been a decade since they'd been separated by events, still, she thought she knew him nearly as well as she knew herself. Maybe better. He had been the golden boy. A cowboy at heart, always wanting to be on the land and have his own ranch one day. And he had succeeded admirably, from what she had seen and heard so far. She was looking forward to learning more about the operation of the ranch in the days ahead.

"What's the matter, Lilybelle? What hurts?" She leaned down awkwardly, thoroughly sick of the crutches always getting in her way. How soon until she was healed and able to maneuver normally? Couldn't be soon enough. So much needed doing. She intended to earn her way, her and Lily's. Not be beholden to anyone. She'd learned that lesson the hard way.

"My tummy hurts, Mommy."

"Where?" Mckenna pressed gently on her four-year-old daughter's abdomen, watching her expression.

She could detect no swelling, no specific area of pain. It could be all the upsets of the past few days. Then arriving to a less-than-warm welcome by Connor's relatives. Brandi had given her and Lily the stink eye a couple of times. She was still complaining to her husband in the bedroom that Mckenna and Lily stood outside of, bashing her brother-in-law for throwing them out. As if. They had been told by Connor to move into the cottage on arrival and apparently ignored his instructions. They had no one to blame but themselves. Mckenna hardened her resolve as she listened to the tirade. The woman was insufferable.

Finally, she stomped into the hallway, carrying a small suitcase and wearing a belligerent expression. "Hope you're happy!" She turned an angry glance on the pair of them waiting patiently for them to vacate the room. "Throws out his own family for the likes of you."

"Apologize!" Connor came out from a room close by, his expression thunderous. "Now! Or so help me, you will both be thrown off my property. I'm not putting up with this."

"Sorry, Connor," Asher said. He had followed his wife

out of the room, loaded down with bags and cases, his expression pale. Perhaps he was learning a side of his wife he didn't know about before?

"Not you. Her," he said, pointing directly at Brandi.

Brandi gave him a murderous glance, but with Connor taking a wide stance in front of her in the hall-way, there was no easy way around him.

"It's okay, Connor. Everyone's on edge. Lily and I are fine." Lily was still crying unfortunately, not proving her words. She had offered them up in efforts to preserve the peace, Lily's sobbing just about breaking her heart.

"I'll not have any of my guests disrespected. Especially by family who should know better, and are only here on my say so."

"We're not charity cases," Asher said, his expression darkening. "We're flesh and blood. Family."

"No, but from what I see you haven't been holding up your end of the bargain either. I wasn't going to get into this tonight, but since you bring it up. With all the work essential for survival in these tough times, you either work or you leave. We clear?"

"Yes, you have been perfectly clear, cousin," Asher said. "We'll hold up our end of the bargain. Right, Brandi?" The man prompted his pouty wife who didn't look nearly as pretty as before with her face all screwed up in anger, her skin splotchy with red patches.

"Yeah, sorry. Now can we go?" She spit out the words.

Connor frowned at her but stepped aside. She flounced by, her actions speaking volumes.

"Sorry about that, Mckenna. Let's get you settled. Is Lily okay?"

"She says her tummy hurts. But I can't tell the source. She might just be upset. I think something to eat and a good night's sleep will make a huge difference."

"Yes. And maybe a nice warm bath with bubbles? I think I have some kicking around."

"Would you like that, princess? A bubble bath that smells nice?"

Lily nodded, her sobs subsiding. With the pressure lowered, she directed her daughter into their new bedroom. It was a grand room, large and spacious, and she knew why the interlopers had chosen it. Skylights. They gave the room a natural glow. A door led off it to what she presumed was the ensuite. A large king-size bed looked inviting with its thick box spring and mattress. There was even a small table and two chairs set in the alcove of a large bay window that faced the front of the property along with plenty of furniture for housing clothing and essentials. A wrap-around balcony with a door leading onto it was a lovely feature and she could only imagine standing there, drinking coffee and staring out at the White Mountains that rose so majestically in the distance. If only the days would calm down, maybe she and Lily could find peace here. A fierce hope built up in her she had no choice but to acknowledge, as it sent its heat coursing through her, making her tingle all over.

"It's grand, Connor. You built a fine place." She smiled at him. Even Lily had stopped crying entirely and had gone exploring, vanishing into the bathroom. No doubt thinking of the promised bubble bath.

Color cheeks turned pink as he acknowledged her praise. "Thanks. I built it by hand, with help of course. I wanted something solid, something that I could pass down to future generations."

"Well, you've more than done that. Congratulations."

The sound of footfalls came racing up the stairs and the man she had recently been introduced to, Sam

Perkins, stood there. He was a good friend to Connor and helped manage the ranch, to her understanding. She was looking forward to meeting his family who also resided at Braveheart.

"Sorry to be the bearer of bad news. But we have a situation and it can't wait. There's a group at the gate demanding an audience. I think the ones that fired a warning shot when you arrived? They say they're staying until you see them."

"Great." Just what he needed. Another incident tonight. He knew keeping his people safe would come at cost, one he was willing to pay. But couldn't a man get a few uninterrupted minutes with the love of his life? He had been tested a great deal already, the trip having taken its toll, down to Golden and back with all the misadventures along the way. The memory brought up another question.

"Did anyone else ask for sanctuary? Sheriff Brady and his family?" He'd met them in the town of Quinton and helped the lawman protect the Quinton Police Detachment from a group of prisoners from the Yellowhead Supermax prison. Connor had been ambushed by a pair of the ex-cons before arriving in Quinton, and in fact had been taking one miscreant there for processing. He'd given Brady a pass onto his ranch if he ever needed to leave his hometown. And from what he'd seen and experienced firsthand there trying to get baby formula for Eve and being shot at with Loch being wounded in the process, it was a good bet he'd decided to take his family to safety.

Sam shook his head at his inquiry. "No. Other than Ty Jasper arriving, no one else has tried to get onto the property."

But they both knew it was only a matter of time. Braveheart was an oasis in the desert. No hiding the fact.

"Okay." Connor raked his hands through his hair, bracing himself. So much for a meal and a shower. It would have to wait. "Best to get this over with." He turned back to Mckenna. "Consider Braveheart your home. Whatever you need, it's yours."

Mckenna's eyes turned glassy, but she managed a wobbly smile. "Thanks, Connor."

He strode from the room, wishing they'd had a bit longer to savor a moment that came seldom in a lifetime. A chance at a new beginning.

———

Diego took a deep breath of satisfaction. Finally, they were getting somewhere. His army was growing daily, the product of the prisons unleashing scores of soldiers into the field. He gathered them up as he marched upward from Mexico through Texas and up through the heartland of America. By the time they arrived in Alaska, he'd be the head of the biggest, most powerful gang to ever hit the state. And they'd be in possession of some very useful weaponry he was having them construct along with a special surprise he'd brought along. *Me, Diego Luis Alberto Martinez, I will be the one in charge, the only one to dictate the future.* Yes, he'd join up with Luther Meech, head of the Kraken cartel. For now, while it served his mission. But in the end, only one of them could be boss. And it wasn't going to be Luther.

SIX
LUTHER

Day 6: Hunting Lodge, Near Anchor, Alaska
    7:13 p.m.

"Where's Luis and the other Thomas?" Thomas asked.

"We gotta come up with another name for you. I can't handle two Thomases. How about just Tom?" And having to say the name Thomas again after seeing the man gunned down by Connor Hale didn't sit well. Though not as bad as the gruesome sight of Joe being beheaded. It still lingered in his mind. A surprise really, considering some of the things he'd been witness to in past years, but maybe it was because it could have been him in the lead snowmobile and the one to be guillotined by the wire strung across the trail? Yeah, simple as that. But who would have thought Hale would have the cajónes for such an action?

"No problem. But it doesn't answer my question. Did they stay behind?"

"Nah. They're gone."

"Shit, that's too bad. Good guys."

The pair of them were out on rounds. Luther wanted to get a sense of the place since he'd been gone. See for himself how the building was coming along. Also, he needed a new lieutenant, and from what he'd seen on first arrival, this new man fit the bill. Almost too much like the old one to be believed, but hey, sometimes life threw you a bone. And the old Thomas had been a great guy. Loyal and hardworking. Knew when to keep his mouth shut. He still had hopes Luis might make it back to Anchor yet, after the snowmobile ambush by the asshole Connor Hale had left him stranded. Luis would understand it was everyman for himself at that moment. Code of the Supermax. At least imprisoned men knew how the real world worked, unlike the do-gooders on the outside who thought everyone would be nice to each other, protect each other, forever. He snorted, just thinking of it. It was everyone for themselves in this brave new world.

"Diego Martinez, head of the Martinez Knights, is headed our way and bringing a small army," he said. He needed to bring Tom up to date on developments. "We need to speed up the building of the barracks. Stockpile more food and medical supplies. You'll be in charge of the night raids in Anchor. Take whatever men and weapons you need, but I want this done yesterday."

"You can count on me, boss." Tom nodded his eager acceptance of the game plan, obviously realizing this was his big chance to make an impression.

"Good." Now that his daughter had made it safely back to him, he was encouraged that Luke would also show up soon. The fact she was pregnant complicated things. And too far along to abort. Sure, hospitals were overloaded, but he could always kidnap a doctor and bring them to the compound at gunpoint to do his bidding. But a grandchild didn't seem half bad. Someone to carry on the family name. Yeah, he could get behind it.

"We need to build an extra room for my kids as well. ASAP. I don't want them thrown in with the others for long." Even as he instructed the man, he had hopes it was only a precaution. He would leave all this to Diego while he took over Braveheart. His kids would stay in the main house at the ranch, safe and sound. But the more building completed here before his new partner Diego arrived, the better. Luther's plans for taking over the ranch were shaping up in his mind and he was almost ready to share them with his crew.

"What's the head count today?" Luther stopped to ask, eyeing the men working on the roof rafters of one of the L-shaped dormitories. Decent building had gone on during his sojourn to Golden, he'd give the ex-prisoners their due. Probably enjoyed being men again after the disrespect of being housed daily in the supermax. Fucking guards were the worst, always on the take. Always looking to beat down any man wanting to be treated like a human being and not an animal.

"Thirty-nine, unless more have shown up since we started our tour."

"Good." Thirty-nine against Hale's small crew of, what had Cheyenne said, less than a dozen adults, half women? It was going to be like taking candy from a baby. The image of seeing the asshole's face once he realized all he had built was going to King Luther sent a coursing satisfaction flowing through him, heating his core. This brave new world was for the taking. "We need all the men we can muster. Is everyone versed in firearms?"

"Oh yeah. No problem there. Our arsenal is well stocked. Each raid has only added to our cache."

"You've done a fine job, Lieutenant."

The man's face cracked open enough to allow a small smile to escape. Tom was a serious man, a man after his own heart. "I won't let you down, sir."

"See that you don't. I don't suffer fools gladly. This opportunity we are being presented with here, at this time in history, it goes without saying it will never come our way again. A chance to do things differently than in the past. Allow natural selection to raise up the oppressed. No longer does it matter if you were born rich, only that you were born to fight to have what should have been yours all along. Your birthright. The strong will take over the earth and make it a better place for those willing to step up. Might is right."

Tom nodded his agreement, his eyes gleaming with interest at Luther's ideology. "Yes, sir. I'm your man. Whatever you need done, consider it accomplished."

"Appreciate that. Some things will be distasteful, no hiding it, but in the end, we will be the survivors, the ones to rebuild the future, shaping it into the way that works best for us. And damn the rest."

SEVEN
CONNOR

Day 6: Braveheart Horse Ranch
  7:15 p.m.

"Sorry about Loch being shot," Sam said as the two of them worked to make the horses comfortable in the barn. Wulver was nearby, intent at staying close. Leaving his loyal hound behind to head down to Golden to rescue Mckenna had been a hard decision, but it was best for the dog. The trip had turned out to be even more dangerous than he'd expected, and he had been expecting the worst, what with Luther shooting an innocent woman just so he could make his getaway. Connor shook his head, the memory scorched forever on his brain, along with others that didn't bear mentioning.

"Yeah, too many innocents are getting harmed." Connor cleaned Loch's wound and reapplied antiseptic and a fresh bandage before administering an antibiotic. The horses were both a bit bruised from the ordeal in the trailer when Connor had no choice but to travel quicker to escape gunfire, but they were alive and giving him a look that spoke volumes about how they felt about their unjust treatment.

He leaned his forehead onto Loch's broad one for a moment, trying to reassure his gallant stallion he had meant no harm as he whispered soothing words of comfort to him. The courageous horses had brought him and his people home. Loch and Finn both deserved the finest treatment. He glanced over at the stalls that normally held the four horses taken by Ty and Cheyanne and felt a terrible sense of loss kick him in the gut. *Please let them be okay.* Horses and children were the innocents in this world. It didn't matter how bad adults had it, it wasn't the same thing. A human understood the bigger picture, a horse did not. It was reliant on its owner to provide for them in a proper manner. He felt the press of the failure to keep his animals safe descend on his shoulders. He had to do better going forward.

"It should never have happened." He gave his friend Sam a quick glance, noting his look of sympathy. Sam loved animals, especially horses and dogs, as much as he did.

"Can't control everything, Connor. It's gotten crazy out there."

After they finished with the horses, Sam and Connor exited the barn and strode across the yard to the main house, both knowing they needed to deal with the group waiting outside the entrance to Braveheart. The unwanted visitors had some explaining to do after their dismal actions earlier in the evening. Even a warning shot could have ricocheted and struck someone. Hurt them or worse. Had everyone forgotten how hard good medical care was to come by? The memory of their angry faces loomed large and center in his mind.

The temperature had plummeted in the past hour while he'd settled his people and dealt with Loch and Finn. Connor pulled his collar up on his parka against the icy cold and shoved his hands in his pockets. As good as it was to be home, he sensed the battle was just beginning. This would be only the first of many groups thinking to show up at his door, demanding to share in what he had built with his own hands. No. Jeopardizing survival could not be allowed to happen. Especially not now with the love of his life, her daughter, plus a newborn orphaned baby in his care. They counted on him to do what had to be done.

Connor stopped on the front porch of the main house and Sam followed suit. "We need to beef up defenses. Prepare for the unexpected. Have every adult share in patrols and defense of the wall. I want everyone efficient in shooting a gun. Now that I'm home, with more bodies to pitch in, we'll get right on it first thing tomorrow," he said.

Sam winced. "Done all I could while you've been gone."

"Not meaning anything by it. But things are only going to escalate. I'm here to help, buddy, not saying anything else. You've had your hands full. What with my cousin and his entitled wife—then Cheyanne taking off. No, I owe you a vote of gratitude for all you've done, Sam. Thank you. If you hadn't held down Braveheart, I couldn't have gotten Mckenna and her daughter and all the others home safely otherwise."

Sam gave him a look of gratitude. "Thanks for that." He cleared his throat. "Now, that being said, how do you want to handle this?"

"No one is coming all this way from town with good intentions. I think we can agree on that?"

"Yeah, no kidding." Sam nodded. "They shot first. Made their position abundantly clear in my opinion."

"They want to share in what we have. Problem is, we can keep everyone alive *here* for a lifetime on everything I've set by including food and medicine, or have all our provisions vanish down a thousand gullets. Be gone in a week if those scavengers or raiders or innocent victims or however they see themselves outside have any say in it. Then our own people pay the price."

Connor took a breath and continued. "Not going to happen on my watch. I didn't plan for all this, made all those sacrifices, poured my heart and soul into this place, just to let others steal it and destroy the very thing that will keep us alive. No, we meet them with force. Let's bring all the men in on it. Everyone armed to the teeth and behind a gun portal."

The 3D built high-defensive wall was his pride and joy. Built to withstand most anything other than a nuclear attack, it had gun portals built in at regular intervals that allowed viewing the outside world as well. A secret tunnel had been built that led out under the road in case of emergency. His last line of defense was the underground bunker under the main house, built from the serious money his mother had left him along with the wall, but he hoped it would never come to that. Living underground for years was not the way human beings were ever meant to live. Money. A useless commodity going ahead, but it had gotten him to this point, able to look after his own now in their greatest hour of need.

"You'll get no argument from me, Connor. I have a wife and two growing boys to think about. Hell, the twins are only five. I can't think of anything I wouldn't do to keep them safe. Laura's pregnant again. If it's a fight they want, it's a fight they get. Too bad Jacob Evans decided to leave on the first day of the event, but he had family in Anchor he had to get back to. We could use all the hands we can get going forward. He said he might come back, bring his family, depending on how it was going in town, but I haven't seen hide or hair of him."

"Yeah, too bad, but I get it. Jacob has a wife and kids to worry about it. Let's bring in Jake and Ben. They both have the right backgrounds and the stomach for this. I've watched them both in action and they are highly trained operatives."

Connor strode back into the house, Wulver at his heels. Both men were in the kitchen now, Ben washing his hands while Jake downed a cup of coffee. They each gave him a look of curiosity.

"I need to talk to you. Get dressed and meet us outside. Bring your weapons."

"I take it this is about our warm welcoming committee at the gate," Jake said, one dark eyebrow raised with a keen look of interest in Connor's direction.

"Right," Ben said, drying his hands on a towel left hanging by the sink. "Be there in a sec."

Both former lawmen donned their outerwear. Then picked up their rifles they had abandoned by the door. They still had their pistols strapped to their waists like gunfighters of old. Connor vowed right then no one would be going around the ranch unarmed from now on. That would be rule number one, followed by rule number two: no child left unattended without an armed adult nearby. Rule number three: don't trust a single soul outside the group. Desperate times brought out the worst in some people. Trouble was, not knowing what was hidden behind those all too human faces and cajoling voices. A trap. Or really someone in need.

Without the means to vet anyone now, they couldn't chance making a mistake and maybe losing everything that provided security for the future. This was going to be the hardest time ever, bar none.

The four of them pushed forward in a straight line up, a few feet between each body. A solid display of manhood, much like Wyatt Earp and his brothers, Morgan and Virgil, striding toward the OK Corral back in the day, he imagined. Connor had read many a western growing up thanks to his closest neighbor Dan Sullivan, an elderly man who now resided on the ranch. He'd read about men walking down the street at high noon to do battle. When Connor glanced at the set expressions on all the men's determined faces, he felt a momentary pride in what these men were going to help him accomplish. As important as anything done in the past when America was won over from the lawless hordes. It was an endless cycle. Build, tear down, rebuild. He'd built his from the ground up, now they'd all have to live through the worst part, destruction of civilization.

"Fast is fine, but accuracy is everything. In a gunfight, you need to take your time in a hurry," Connor said, earning a curious glance from the other men. "A quote from Wyatt Earp."

"Wait up," a voice called from behind them and Connor turned to see Luke and his grandpa Dan coming toward them, shotguns in hand.

Dan spoke up. It was obvious he had overheard Connor's words. "Right. He's the guy who also said; *no wise man ever took a handgun to a gunfight.*"

"Good to see you, Dan. Luke." Had it only been six days ago since he'd shown the teenager, Cheyanne's brother and Dan's grandson, how to build a smokeless Dakota fire hole up near God's River? The day he'd lost his father to the EMP event on their annual fishing trip pushed hard at Connor, sweeping him away for a moment of intense grief for the death of his dad before he could push it away. But now was not the time for grieving. There may never be the luxury of time for grieving ever again. At least not in his lifetime.

"Happy to see you made it back in one piece," Dan said. The old man was a fine sight, though the strains of the past days were obvious on his weathered, wrinkly skin. But his eyes were still alert though the blue of his irises had long faded.

"I got all those new westerns to read you dropped off last week. They were calling my name," Connor said, clapping the older man on the shoulder while making light of the dangers he'd faced during the past days. A man keeps his burdens to himself.

"The men of the Old West, the ones who understood the code, knew how to handle themselves. I take it we're going to deal with the rabble at the gate. Noisy, persistent bastards, I'll give them that." Loud shouts resounded in the distance, still expressing the angry tensions of earlier.

Dan was never a man afraid to speak his mind, something Connor greatly admired. The pair of them had enjoyed many a conversation in the past about the state of things. He was the first to mention about the sentient computer in Washington naming itself Eastwood after the legendary actor Clint Eastwood. He'd shared the news the same day he'd asked Connor to look out for his grandkids, saying he didn't have long for this world. In fact, Dan and his wife Jean were getting on and he'd promised to do the best by them. And now his granddaughter had taken off, adding another wrench to Connor's plans to keep them all safe.

"Sorry about Cheyanne," Connor said.

Dan's expression turned bleak. "We have to get her back. Jean says she's pregnant. She was waiting to talk to her about it, but then she took off with that Jasper kid. It's too dangerous out there for her to be with her dad, which is where she is no doubt headed. He's moved into a hunting lodge up north. You remember, the one the old mayor, Buck Duffy, owned when your mom and him had it out and he lost? You know as well as me what Luther's capable of, Connor. Promise me, you'll get her home safe and sound." Dan sounded desperate and he could see how shaken the old man was pleading the case for his granddaughter.

"What? I didn't know she was pregnant." The news was unsettling. Shocking in such a young girl. And an added complication. He could no more ignore the young teen's plight than turn away Mckenna's daughter. Unthinkable. And now the young woman had a baby on the way. Perhaps it went some way to explaining why she'd been so prickly of late of not only Connor, but her grandparents as well. "You have my word, Dan. We will get your granddaughter back. Whatever it takes."

"Thank you. I'm sorry she's been so hard on you." Dan's expression softened at his words. He didn't know in the moment how he was going to accomplish it, but he did know he'd do his best to fulfill the promise. Luther's daughter or not, she deserved a chance to get her life on track and there was no way it would happen if she was staying up at the hunting lodge with all those ex-prisoners converging on the place. It was a magnet for low lifers, always had been, as he remembered the former mayor and his nefarious ways. No, he wouldn't wish the situation on anyone, let alone a pregnant teen, even if it was her father she was trying to reach. Hell,

Luther hadn't been this far north in days, having spent time chasing after him and Mckenna in Golden, meaning he wasn't even there to protect her the little he was capable of. Cheyanne's plight had just moved to the top of his priority list for where to apply all his energies and resources next. The thought added more weight to his steps. First he'd deal with the miscreants at the gate. Then he'd be free to rescue Dan's granddaughter.

"She's a teenager. Isn't that their job?" Connor said, making light of Cheyanne's treatment of him in the past. She had spirit to spare. In some ways she reminded him of Mckenna as a teenager. But it was a serious matter now to protect the young girl from herself and the thought hastened his steps even further as he led the way down the roadway to the wall.

The angry shouts of the townspeople only grew louder as the five of them finished the trek to the gate. Connor took a moment to admire his 3D rebar-enforced wall. Ten feet high with a triple row of steel wire strung out all along the top adding another three feet, its sharp metal barbs menacing as they glinted against the sunlight. A person would tear themselves up something fierce if they attempted to climb over it. It was also three feet thick with viewing ports every twenty feet, large enough to shoot through. No different from the original military forts that once protected America. Right now, he wished he'd gone for an even higher wall, but even though his pockets were deep, they weren't deep enough to afford the added cost for such a vast undertaking, not with everything else he'd had done at the time as well. Creating the underground shelter had pretty much emptied his bank account.

"I'll do the talking," Connor said. "They need to see how serious I am about keeping what I have built for my own people. Only way I know to get them to leave. Back me up if they try to push their way in. But don't shoot unless—"

"I don't see why you need to open the gate." Dan shook his head, immediately jumping on his plan, his mouth set in a grim line. "Why not tell them to leave or we will make them leave?"

Luke's eyes widened at Dan's words. "What do you mean, Grandpa?"

"Those people out there are in the way of us getting your sister back. They are taking up our precious time, threatening violence. Hell, they've already proved it by firing off shots. Do you care more about them than Cheyanne? Those people just want to take what we have. They don't care a fig about us. They'd trample us to death in a heartbeat to steal our food."

Luke shook his head, his lower lip trembling. "Of course not. I want Cheyanne back as bad as you."

Connor had never seen this side of his neighbor before. But he understood. And the old man had a point. If he did the wrong thing today, got himself or one of the others shot, who would get Cheyanne back? There had to be fifty people gathered out there, maybe more by now.

"Let me check on what the deal is." He stepped up to a portal and opened the viewing slot. Because the walls were so thick, he couldn't see how many were milling around outside the gates, but he could see the glint of drawn weapons. Yes, Dan was right. They would storm the gates as soon as he opened it.

EIGHT
CONNOR

Day 6: Braveheart Horse Ranch
   7:59 p.m.

"Okay, new plan. I'll warn them to leave. Give them a five-minute time limit. Then if they don't, we lob some flashbangs over and get them to disperse." It wasn't what he wanted. He was more a meet face-to-face kind of guy, but his people counted on him. He'd be risking his life soon enough going after Cheyanne. This could be handled far easier than her rescue.

"Now you're talking," Dan said, a grim look of approval etched on his wrinkled face.

"Not like there's a manual for this kind of weird situation," Sam spoke up, shaking his head.

"Actually, there is. Government produced a document for keeping private citizens under control by rounding them up and taking them to camps back when nuclear war threatened in the past," Jake said, his expression cold and shut down. "Not on my watch. What you have here, Connor. Never risk it by allowing anyone, government or otherwise, to invade your property. If Dan hadn't spoke up, I would have."

Ben nodded with agreement. "Jake's right."

Connor pondered logistics for a moment. "I need a bullhorn. They're getting louder. You wait here. I have one." He gestured at Wulver to stay put, then took off at a quick jog back toward the house, visualizing where he had stored the old-fashioned device. It would amplify his voice, allowing it to be heard over the caterwauling outside the wall.

He hurried inside the attached garage to the main house and located the horn hanging halfway down the side wall on a hock with a quick glance, exactly where he expected it to be. He also filled his jacket pockets with the gear he would need if the crowd didn't disperse. He then raced back down the driveway to the gate. The sense of time slipping away pressed in on him from every corner, giving him the focus to see clearly what was only right before him now.

"Okay, I'm set." He took a deep breath, considered his words, and spoke slowly and clearly into the device. "This is Connor Hale, owner of the ranch. You all knew my father, Chief of Police Josh Hale and my mother Anna in her fight for justice. It's time for all of you to leave my property. There is *nothing* here for you. If you don't disperse in five minutes, be advised we will take action in the form of flashbangs and tear gas to move you on. I don't want to see anyone hurt, but be advised I will do what I have to. This is not a negotiation. Again, there is *nothing* here for any of you. Go home. Stay safe."

A few moments of dead silence while they all waited, thinking of what would happen next.

A cacophony of sounds erupted beyond the wall,

even angrier than before. Wulver began barking, adding to the confusion. He was a prized guard dog, worth his weight in gold many times over.

"Seems to have done the job," Jake quipped. No one liked this, it went without saying.

"We'll give 'em five. Maybe reality will sink in by then. They aren't getting in, and standing outside our gate's only going to waste their time. Moving on and choosing another option is their only choice," Connor said.

"Where will they go, Grandpa?" Luke asked, his eyes troubled.

Dan grimaced, trying to hide his emotions like the rest of them were doing. "Anywhere but here. You want them stealing your food? Leaving all your family and friends to starve?"

Luke looked down at his feet, appearing crushed by his grandpa's warning.

A harsh reality had hit sooner rather than later. Too many had ignored the warnings of an event like this coming at some point, meaning too many were unprepared. Government camps might work for them. But definitely not for his people. The kind of hierarchy that would take over in such a place would devastate most people. Set them back. Maybe for years. Power corrupting absolutely was far more than just as saying. It was a reality, and had been such the beginning of time.

The loud arguing as people tried to shout over others continued unabated as the clock ticked downward. What was the matter with them? Why waste energy on a lost cause? No way were they going to be able to breech the wall, not without building a huge ramp, which was a possibility of course, but one he could easily blow up before it became a problem with the dynamite he had stashed away. The wall was too strong and thick to be conquered without specialized equipment all needing tremendous power to run. Power the world was now short of. Barring an advanced form of weaponry which was an unlikely scenario arriving at Braveheart's gate when there were other places in warmer climes to choose from, they would be safe for many years to come. He reminded himself *this too shall pass* as his nerves began to fray from listening to the voices of the desperate.

"It's been at least five minutes, right?" Jake said, his mouth twitched to the side. The continued shouting was getting on everyone's nerves.

"Yeah, time to let them know we stand behind our words. Let's check the other nearby portals, see how far they have strung themselves out," Connor said. The men moved down the wall at regular intervals and opened the viewing ports.

"No one here," Jake called out. He'd moved the farthest away, heading north. The town of Anchor was to the south and east.

"Still behind this one," Ben checked in, pointing at the wall, one portal down from Connor's which meant a distance of twenty-five feet as the openings had been placed at regular intervals.

"Not down here," Dan called out from the east portal he'd chosen.

Connor strode toward Ben and handed over a couple of flashbangs and a slim canister of tear gas. "You got a good arm?"

"Hell, yeah."

"Good, we'll lob them over at my signal. Then we move away to avoid any residue. If this doesn't work, we send over a second round."

Connor moved into position, then gave Ben the nod, and in unison, they pulled the pins from the devices and threw them up and over the electrified razor wire powered by solar. The loud sounds of the flashbangs going off were somewhat muffled by the wall, but still ear piercing enough to make Luke cover his ears.

"Move back." He gestured at the men. "The tear gas has a tendency to drift."

The stench of the gas quickly followed as the group followed his orders.

"What do we do now?" Luke asked, his eyes wide.

"We wait and see if they have a lick of common sense and head back the way they came. Or move further on. I don't care which, but I need them to get the message. Braveheart protects its own."

Luke stared at Connor, his expression suggesting his mind was dealing with something heavy. He was a good kid, an eager worker with a caring heart. He promised himself before he'd left Anchor to rescue Mckenna and Lily in Golden, he would spend more time with him and he intended to live up to the promise. "Do you think my sister's okay?"

"I don't think Luther would hurt her, if that's what you're asking." He couldn't promise for certain that it was not the case knowing what the bastard was capable of, but he deemed it unlikely. However, she was also in the company of ex-prisoners from the toughest prison in Alaska, the Yellowhead Supermax, notorious for housing the worst of the worst. But he wasn't going to say it to her brother who obviously loved and cared for his sister.

"My dad, he did things. Cheyanne just won't believe any of it." Luke still looked troubled, chewing on his bottom lip. "Do you think stuff like that, you know, bad stuff, is it like...catchy?"

Though it was awkwardly put, Connor understood what the troubled teen was asking. "No, I don't. I think it's a choice a man or a woman makes." He cleared his throat, sensing more needed to be said. "My mother went through a period of time when some in Anchor blamed her for my sister Tia's disappearance. Said the sins of the father were visited on his offspring. And the time-worn idiocy of the apple not falling far from the tree. Her father was executed for the murder of her mom and attempted murder of her." The scars his mother bore on her body and her mind came back full force at his words. "And she went on to become one of the biggest slayers of injustice the world has ever seen."

"Wow, the great Anna Hale went through what I'm going through?" Luke's eyes nearly bugged out of his head as realization hit home.

"Yeah, pretty much the same situation."

Luke nodded, his body taking on a firmer stance as he stood up straighter. "We're going to rescue her, right? Real soon?"

"Soon as I can arrange it, buddy. First thing I'm going to do."

NINE
CHEYANNE

Day 6: Hunting Lodge, Near Anchor, Alaska
    9:44 p.m.

The sounds of something crashing to the floor in one of the other rooms woke Cheyanne up from a deep sleep. So deep she came to her senses slowly, her blurry eyes adjusting to her surroundings with protest. She'd only been asleep for a short while and it took a moment for her to recognize where she was. Not in her bedroom at the ranch like normal, but at the hunting lodge with barely a few square feet of living space in the women's room. She lay on a narrow bed that didn't smell too clean, the only thing standing between her and the next sleeper was a blanket thrown over a yellow tie rope fastened at both ends by a nail to the wall. A freakin' lousy situation.

Then events of the day came storming back in and she groaned with grief and despair as she relived the fear and horror of what had happened to Ty on the journey.

Seeing his prone body lying on the road, covered in blood. Tears leaked from her eyes and she rubbed them away, the horrible images quickly followed by anger, mostly directed at adults for causing the shitty situation.

She held her hands over her ears as shouting erupted somewhere in the log structure, turning over and facing the wall, pillow over her head. *Shut up!* She screamed the words in her mind, wishing she were still back at Braveheart. Not that she would ever admit her stupid mistake to a living soul. If only Luke had come with her, things would make sense. But even her own brother had abandoned her.

Bang. Bang. The eruption of gunshots focused her mind on the present. What was going on? Could a bullet find its way through the wall and hit her? She trembled with fear at the thought that if it did, it might harm her baby. She had to try leaving right now. But when she stood up on the bed and tried to open the window, she found it nailed shut. No way out. She'd have to try escaping out of a different room.

She peeked around the blanket and found the room empty. Thankfully, it was too early for the partyers to be in bed. She could hear it going on strong though at the front of the lodge with peals of female laughter and the loud, rumbly male voices. Where was her dad in all this?

She pulled on the parka she'd left at the foot of the bed and her boots, then crept across the room and slowly opened the door. It squeaked, making her cringe. Had someone heard? She wanted to check for a back door. No point in staying here. It was too dangerous. And her dad hadn't lived up to his word. She refused to live in squalor with these pigs. With a bit of luck, maybe she could even find one of the horses to ride home on. And maybe some of the stuff she'd taken. Then she could pretend it had all been Ty's idea and she was bringing it back to them. Her mind filled with hope at the idea that all would be forgiven and forgotten in no time. *I'll try a little harder from now on if you let me get safely home, I promise.* She sent the prayer out to the universe, desperate for it to be answered.

She increased her speed when she found no one lurking in the hallway, making a bee line for the back of the lodge, legs pumping. Cheyanne swiveled her head back and forth at the end of the hall, looking for a way out, checking which way led to the exit.

"What are you doing?" a male voice called out, freezing her in place for a second. He was coming toward her, rifle over his shoulder, his outside clothes suggesting he'd just come in the back door. She could smell the fresh Alaskan air emulating from his jacket and see the frost crusting his unkept beard.

"Going outside for some fresh air. I'm feeling sick." An easy feign. She knew she had to look bad. She'd never been a pretty crier. Was anybody really? She mentally snorted. Maybe if it was faked with big crocodile tears.

"Cheyanne Meech, right? Your dad said you needed to stay put. Too dangerous outside for a young girl like you."

"Too dangerous inside," she retorted. Why did this asshole have to show up now? He stood between her and freedom. If freedom had an odor, it was the fresh breeze coming off the White Mountains.

"It would be my hide if anything happens to Luther's little girl. So, I suggest you head back to your bedroom right now. Open a window if you need fresh air."

"It won't open," she countered.

He grimaced; his eyes filled with indecision. Then he relented. "Okay, let me see what I can do."

"Which room are you in?" He was leading the way back down the hallway and turned to ask the question.

"The women's area."

She followed him into the bedroom, then watched as he tried pushing up the sash on the window frame. "It's stuck," he grunted.

Cheyanne rolled her eyes, knowing he couldn't see her make a face because he was staring at the wall. Like this was news. "I think you need a hammer. Someone nailed it shut."

"I don't have a hammer." He stepped away, preparing to leave.

"Could you maybe *get* one? I heard a lot of building going on earlier today. Surely there are lots of hammers around here somewhere."

"I don't have time. Ask your dad or someone else. I'm finished with my duty for the day." He had to be thinking about the fun others were having without his presence. They could both hear clear enough the shenanigans going on at the front of the lodge with the bouts of silly laughter and feminine screams of fake protest. At least she hoped it was put on by the women. She pushed the worry from her mind and gave the disgusting man as big a smile as she could manage.

"It won't take long and I would be grateful for the help. What's your name?"

"James. Yeah. How grateful?" His eyes crept over her body, making her feel like she'd been slimed.

"I don't think my dad would appreciate your being paid more than my offering you a thank you, James," she said pointedly.

"Don't you know where you are, baby doll? This ain't the Garden of Eden. Everything's up for barter. This is Sodom and Gomorrah with a side of Caligula's and

Nero's Rome. No holds barred." He snickered a bark of self-satisfied laughter at his smarmy wit. "And there ain't nobody playing the fiddle."

"Yeah, I know where I am. And it's under my dad's protection."

"Good luck with opening the window." He stepped away, moving around the curtain and heading for the open door.

"No, please." She rushed to stop him, grabbing frantically at his jacket. "I need your help. I'm suffocating! I need fresh air. My baby needs fresh air."

"What baby? I don't see no baby."

"I haven't had it yet."

He shook his head and grumbled. "I'll see what I can do, okay. Wait here. This crew will eat you for a late-night snack." He snickered again and exited the room.

Cheyanne was too antsy to sit down, and she began to pace the room between the rows of cots. The beds were unmade, looking like the partiers just crawled in when exhaustion or being drunk made them pass out. What a freakin' way to live. She was more and more certain she had made the worst mistake of her life, coming to live with her dad. Not that any of this was his fault. How was he to know the world was going to be turned upside down? Or that so many lowlifes were going to descend on the lodge?

She waited impatiently for as long as she could take it, wondering if the asshole was making the hammer or pry bar required to open the window. *I gotta get out of here.*

TEN
LUTHER

Day 6: Hunting Lodge, Near Anchor, Alaska
  10:19 p.m.

"Can I speak with you, sir?" James asked.

The ex-prisoner approached Luther as he sat between two women on one of the sofas. Luther was determined to show his status with double the numbers anyone else was allowed. The guard's expression was respectful, which was why he allowed him to approach him while he was otherwise engaged. One of the two females fighting for his attention had her hand down his pants while the other had doffed her top to give him a better view of the goods she was offering. Both wanted to be his queen. Of course, neither would be given the chance, they weren't anything like Hope Bredeson, but he was enjoying the tryouts.

"Say your piece," Luther said. He eyed the young guard standing in front of him. Mid to late twenties, up-and-comer who took on extra shifts to show his support and demonstrate he was onboard. Luther could use more like him.

"It's about your daughter," James said, his voice hesitant.

"What about her?" Luther said and sat up. He shoved the women away.

"She was complaining the room was too stuffy and wants the window opened. It's nailed shut."

"And for good reason. Have you opened it?"

"No, nothing like that. Just thought I should inform you."

"You did right." Was Cheyanne thinking of leaving her old dad or was it just what she said it was? The lodge was stuffy since he'd ordered all the vulnerable entry points closed off. Could be a coincidence. But he needed to keep a closer eye on her.

"You still on duty?"

"Sure, if you need me to be?" Meaning the guard had finished his shift, but wasn't going to let the boss down if he wanted more of him. Smart.

"Stand guard outside her room until I say different. Don't engage her. Got it."

"Yes, sir."

"I got room in my organization for men who know how to follow orders to the letter. They advance quicker."

James nodded once more, understanding clear in his eyes before he exited the common room. Luther turned his energies back to the pair of women. Cheyanne would learn her place in time. Respect his choices for her without question. Only way to keep her safe was here, with him. Maybe she wasn't looking to escape but just wanted fresh air like she said, but Luther wasn't taking any chances. His children were important to him, a living promise of his genes making it into the future. And now she was pregnant, he was making damn sure she stayed put. He'd have to find her a better place to stay though, meaning in the morning he'd get the men working on a private room for her. Then have others make a foraging trip to Anchor for baby shit. That should keep his little girl happy.

He turned his attention back on the two females, his mind at ease.

"Let's head into the back. Any room except my daughter's."

Both women jumped to their feet before leading him down the hallway to an unoccupied bedroom. He left behind men and women in different stages of having or preparing to have sex, finding it quite acceptable for his men to engage in full view of each other. Hell, it probably turned them on being exhibitionists. They were starved for female company after being in prison. But he was the leader and needed to keep the edge. Fawning on him in the common room was one thing, riding him cowgirl style was quite another.

Everyone was now naked in the trio. He was being entertained by the show he'd asked for, enjoying a little girl-on-girl action before performing himself, when another burst of gunfire erupted. He ignored it. Just another night at the lodge.

ELEVEN
MCKENNA

Day 6: Braveheart Horse Ranch
   10:23 p.m.

Mckenna checked in on her daughter, grateful to see she was sleeping peacefully, her tiny body barely noticeable in the huge king-size bed. She closed the bedroom door quietly and headed down the staircase using the annoying crutches. All the adults were congregated in the kitchen, sitting around the large wooden table. Faraday was feeding the baby and the others were drinking coffee. Connor looked up when she slipped into the room and patted a chair beside him for her to sit on. She leaned the crutches against a cupboard and eased into her seat.

"Mckenna. Good you can join us. We're just having an impromptu meeting. That's Laura, Sam's wife, and Dan Sullivan, Luke and Cheyanne's grandfather."

"Cheyanne's the young girl who ran away yesterday,

right?" Mckenna noted Laura sitting beside Sam with her thick brown hair pulled into a ponytail and bright blue eyes and the much older Dan with the white wispy hair. Luke was ginger-haired, a boy on the cusp of becoming a man in his mid-teens. This current crisis would make all the children grow up quicker than had happened in generations unfortunately.

"You heard."

"Faraday told me earlier. Nice to meet you Laura, Dan, Luke." Laura was obviously a good woman, her expression welcoming and warm as was Dan's. Luke looked at her shyly, then down at the table. He appeared a sweet-natured boy and she wondered what his sister Cheyanne was like. She'd picked a bad time to run away.

"You as well, Mckenna," Laura said. "I'm sorry you got hurt on the journey."

Mckenna shrugged, not wanting to draw attention to it. "It's healing fine. I should be able to get rid of the crutches altogether soon."

"Dan's wife Jean is looking after Laura's twin boys. You'll likely meet her tomorrow. She makes all the bread for us," Connor explained.

"I want to help as well. Whatever you need me to do. I have a four-year-old, Lily, but she can help me some and at other times I can babysit all the children, if that works for you, Laura."

"Cheyanne was helping with babysitting along with Jean. And we hope to get her back with us soon. But I could certainly use assistance in the greenhouse and garden. Then there's clothes washing, meal preparation—"

"I love to cook. I could make all our meals here, if you like. Not like the kitchen isn't big enough. Communal kitchens work well, save time and resources, according to my Grandma McTavish."

"Good idea," Laura beamed. "I like this girl, Connor. We need more good women going forward."

Mckenna warmed under her praise. She was so thankful to now have a good place for her and Lily to stay. And feeling part of a community, offering her help where and when she could, made her feel more useful and better than she had in years. It might be too early to call it, but hope filled her that she had found her new home here at the ranch. She sat up straighter. "You said something about Cheyanne coming home soon?"

"Yes. She was encouraged to leave the ranch by her father. Luther, the man who broke out of prison just before the EMP event. He's probably said whatever it took to get Cheyanne to follow him up to the hunting lodge. Luke was sharing that she even took up a number of two-way radios along with the four horses."

Luke looked downcast at the revelation.

Connor gave him a look of sympathy and laid a hand briefly on the boy's shoulders. "No one's fault but Luther's. We need to get her back here with us. All the ex-prisoners from the supermax are headed up there. It's no place for a young, pregnant teen."

"No kidding. Is that what this meeting is about? Rescuing her?" Mckenna shuddered at the idea of Dan's granddaughter headed into such a situation. Her father was certifiable for suggesting she should travel there where he was also encouraging ex-prisoners to go and stay as well. The situation spelled nothing but trouble.

"Partly. We also need to establish some ground rules to keep everyone safe. Simple but effective things like wearing a gun at all times and never leaving the property by yourself. Or leave a child unguarded. Things will only get worse for the outside world now, no telling what others will do to try to take what we have. We turned away a group tonight wanting to invade Braveheart. They were encouraged to leave, but it took more than just a verbal warning. I'm afraid it's only the beginning. We have to ask ourselves how far we are willing to go to protect what is ours, to keep our people fed for the hard years to come?"

Sam nodded, taking Laura's hand in his. A gesture Mckenna found romantic and endearing at the same time. "I would do anything to keep Laura's and the boys' lives intact. Whatever it takes. Goes without saying."

More nods around the table proved everyone was on the same page.

Dan cleared his throat and placed his hands, palms down, on the table. "I'm all in favor of whatever we need to do to get my granddaughter back. To think she's stuck in the den of vipers turns my stomach. I know she's impulsive, but she's young. Headstrong. She'll learn one day and look back at her former self and won't believe the stuff she pulled. But that takes time, a luxury we don't have. If we don't look out for the young ones, who will?"

"We're all on the same page then. Time to plan how to get Cheyanne home," Connor said. "I think we should take The Shark, park it a distance away, then use night vision to scope out the place. I will warn you; Luther has many more bodies than we do. Hardened criminals with nothing to lose. This is coming to be a dangerous mission. Think about that before you volunteer to come along."

"I'm going," Luke said. "Cheyanne's my sister. I should have told you, Grandpa, that she was thinking of leaving. I'm sorry. This is all my fault." The young teen hung his head and Mckenna's heart went out to him.

"It's no one's fault at the ranch, Luke. It's not your burden to carry. It's Luther's for pushing Cheyanne to do his dirty work of stealing resources from us. Encouraging her with a pipe dream."

"I had a hand in it as well, son," Sam spoke up. "I let her talk to Luther that day when he came by to see her. It was probably then he hatched his plan. So, no blaming yourself. Okay? We will fix this."

Luke nodded. Relief was obvious on his flushed face.

Jake spoke up. "Count me in."

"Me as well," Ben said.

"I can't walk long distances, but I could stay with The Shark and be the driver," she offered.

"No. You're needed more here."

"I want to do my part—" She began to protest, then stopped when she got a certain look from Laura, seeming to ask her to stand down.

"The time will come when you will be called upon to defend Braveheart, Mckenna. For now, I think it best for everyone to leave you, Laura, Faraday, and Jean here to look after the place and keep the children safe," Connor said in a firm, no nonsense tone. Mckenna remembered their first argument had been over her not wanting to take orders from anyone ever again. But this was Connor, the man trying to see the big picture now and how best to keep his people safe. Perhaps now was not the time to challenge it. She did have a child to think about, and really, how much help could she be until she was off the crutches? Which couldn't be too soon in her opinion.

"You don't need four women to keep four children

safe," Faraday spoke up. "I'm going. I'm a crack shot with a gun and I have less to lose than the other women."

"The baby has taken to you," Connor pointed out.

"Eve's less than a week old. She wouldn't remember me if something happens. So that's no excuse. And both Mckenna and Laura are quite capable of looking after her." Faraday looked everyone in eye in turn, then said flat out. "I'm going, and that's that."

TWELVE
CONNOR

Day 6: Braveheart Horse Ranch
   10:45 p.m.

Connor nodded at Faraday's declaration that she was going no matter what on the raid at the lodge to bring Cheyanne home. He understood more than she knew. After her ordeal being locked in the cabin against her will, she needed to take charge of her life. And what better way than helping others in a similar situation? Yes, Cheyanne had gone of her own accord, but she was under a delusion that her dad was a decent man put upon by the system. She didn't know the real Luther Meech like the outside world did. Plus, she was a teenager with all the hormonal changes that entailed and a young person trying to find her way in the world. Throw in a pregnancy and it got even more complicated.

"Fine. You're in. I say we get a few hours rest, rise at around three a.m. We'll arrive at the cabin around 4 a.m. when everyone should be asleep. I expect guards to be on duty. We need to see where she's staying. The first day will be watching and doing recon, gathering intelligence. Check out the patterns. The lodge is surrounded by forest, tucked in a shallow valley. I know the area well from taking groups out on survivalist trips, acting as their guide. Sam too," Connor said. The expression on the faces of the men told him they agreed with his plan. Yes, doing recon put Cheyanne at more risk as it delayed the operation, but going in without any intel was suicide. He needed to see how this group of ex-cons operated. Their strengths and their weaknesses.

"Sounds good," Jake said. "We're going to be outnumbered, but we can use the element of surprise to our advantage when we go in. No way will they expect us to be attacking their stronghold."

"Gonna need balls of steel for this one," Ben quipped. "Fortunately, I am well prepared."

Connor was hard pressed not to chuckle. A few half-hidden smiles erupted, lighting the mood. Yes, it was going to be a dangerous enterprise, no hiding it, but a certain laissez-faire attitude helped.

"Then we'd better head for bed," Dan said. Much as the elderly man wanted to rescue his granddaughter, it was obvious it was already taking its toll. Dan's skin was gray, his movements a bit shaky. But no telling the man to back down. Not with what was at stake. If only Sheriff Brady and his family had made it, he'd have another lawman on his side.

"Dan's right. We'll meet up in the garage just before three. I've got a cache of extra weapons and ammunition stored there, same as a few strategic spots around the ranch. I'll make everyone familiar with them over the coming days. No one goes around unarmed. Okay, meeting adjourned."

He turned off the lights as soon as everyone exited the main house, watching through the window as the men and women dispersed to their homes. Then turned toward Mckenna when he realized she was standing at his side. Their eyes locked. A certain look on her face drew his full attention and he raised a hand up to cup her cheek, unaware he was even going to do it until he felt her warm, soft flesh against his fingertips.

"You are so beautiful," he murmured. She leaned into him then, her eyes holding a promise of more.

"Let's go to bed," she said. "I know you need your rest, but I want you to hold me, Connor, tonight."

The invitation was almost his undoing. To hold Mckenna in his arms once more was something he never thought he'd ever get to experience again in this lifetime. He swallowed hard before nodding. "I can't believe you're home, here, with me. It doesn't seem real."

"I'm just flesh and blood like any other woman."

"Never like any other woman. You were everything to me, back then."

"And now?"

"So much more, if that's even possible." He stroked the side of her face, enjoying the velvety feel of her porcelain skin. Then buried his face in her hair, breathing in the scent that was all hers alone. The womanly fragrance brought welcomed memories of an earlier time, a far easier one. Even if it didn't always feel like it back then.

They embraced for a long moment, then broke apart. She took his hand and led him up the stairs, stopping in front of his former bedroom.

"I need to check on Lily." He could see the quandary in her eyes. After days of her and Lily being inseparable, it would be difficult not to be in the same room at night, safe as she was at Braveheart. Or as safe as anyone barring the president and his entourage in this new world.

Hard as it was, he offered a quick solution, sensing it was too soon for more. "We can both do that and keep her company tonight. I just want to hold you, Mckenna."

THIRTEEN
SHERIFF BRADY

Day 6: Quinton, Alaska
   11:13 p.m.

The sounds of gunfire woke Brady from the first solid sleep he'd fallen into since the crisis hit. He rubbed his eyes and sat up groggily, momentarily unaware of where he was. Exhaustion lay heavy on him and he knew he'd only been asleep a couple of hours. He was in his own home, having abandoned guarding the jail the day before to focus all his efforts on keeping his family safe. Ever since a group of armed men claiming to be from the government had shown up two days before, stating their instructions were to help guard the town of Quinton and to gather all the supplies and stash them in the town hall, he'd been on high alert. Though the men had credentials proving they had indeed worked for the state, they weren't on the level, and his every instinct screamed danger.

He needed to get his family away. Problem was, the

men were guarding the entrances to and from town, not letting anyone leave or enter. They'd been systematically entering homes and demanding resources, carting them away in wagons. Anyone who protested was quickly dealt with. It was only a matter of time until they were at his doorstep, demanding he hand over what he'd set by. And no way would he allow that to happen. Yes, they had let the church set up a feeding station. But how long was the food going to last with more and more of the so-called soldiers showing up daily?

"Go back to sleep, hon," he said. His wife Marilyn murmured at his side, patting his arm sleepily. But it was no use, so he decided he might as well let his wife get some rest because he knew he'd be tossing and turning for the rest of the night. He got out of bed and pulled on his clothes, then tied his boots before sliding his Glock into its holster. He picked up his rifle and headed into the living room, setting it down nearby.

He needed to make a plan. Brady pulled out the handwritten pass Connor Hale had given him a few days ago, smoothed the folds, and reread the words that stated that he and his family would be allowed into Braveheart Horse Ranch. Yes. He had a destination in mind. Much as he hated the thought of abandoning his town, the place he'd lived all his married and working life, his first obligation was to his family. Besides, the group calling themselves SGs, or State Guardians, was in charge of the jail now, saying his help was no longer required. But far as he could tell, they were only locking up anyone who protested their mandate. Yeah, they were no more SGs then he was Santa fucking Claus.

He suspected they were also brain-damaged for the most part from the implanted comms so many had used before the disaster, turning themselves into the closest thing to zombies the world had ever known. He didn't trust the implant comms though they were the most reliable brain-net implant device invented with direct brain-to-brain contact, like thousands of others also mistrusted and instead opting for a small bug in their ear canal. Turned out to be a far safer option to mind speak with others. God, he missed the conveniences of his other life. The simple pleasures of things being reliable and doing what they were supposed to.

Would there ever be a time again when children believed in the jolly, present-gifting man? Maybe. But children were going to grow up far too quickly now, entirely opposite from what his two kids, Layla and Jamie, had experienced in their short lifetimes. Already they were having difficulty absorbing the entirety of the situation. Still complaining about all the changes to their lives, only doing the bare minimum to get by. That had to stop. The days and weeks ahead were fraught with danger and each person had to dig down deep and give the best of themselves.

He glanced at the four bug-out bags he'd assembled the past day since he'd seen the writing on the wall with the SGs. They held everything he thought would aid them on the journey. Everything from a simple water purifying system to prevent intestinal problems to nutrient-dense food bars. He'd don the heaviest pack of course, carrying extra ammunition, a field cleaning kit for weapons that had been chosen for their easy dismantling, a medical kit, and tarps to shelter them while they slept. Each person would have to carry some water and an extra blanket and clothing, hygiene supplies, and they'd need to wear good footwear. He could just imagine Layla protesting at not being allowed her curling iron or her fancy high-heeled boots, but blisters had to be prevented. And in this she would listen to her father. He may have been too soft in the past, but that was over.

Brady tried to imagine his children wearing the extra weight, walking down the road a hundred miles to the ranch. Braveheart was up near Anchor. It would take at least a week to ten days to cover the distance, and that was if they got lucky. Well, he'd just have to put up with the whining and complaining. Once they got tired enough, maybe it would stop, he could only hope. It was mostly his fault they had been raised in such an easy existence. Hell, he'd had a smart house built with every convenience imaginable to man thinking that made him a great provider. Now it was all useless. He'd have been better off putting his money and resources into teaching his children how to survive in the wilderness like so many Alaskans did, taken them camping, make them learn they could rely on each other for support in hard time. Ah, but this was no time for regrets.

At least he had a way out for his family. Connor Hale was a man of his word, he'd seen that when he'd put in his appearance in town and helped him with a situation, dealing with the men trying to break out a prisoner in his jail and another man looking to harm his own family, driven to desperation only hours into the disaster. Connor had been on his way to Golden to rescue a woman and her child, but had taken the time to stop and help him. He knew now how much that must have cost the man. He was the son of the legendary police chief, Josh Hale. A lawman stricken down on the first day of the event. How many other good men had been lost, victims of this insanity?

A sudden blast imploded the air and Brady lumbered to his feet, pulling back the drape to check the street outside. Damn it. Another fire had broken out a couple of streets away. And all the fire-bots and police-bots were down, destroyed in the initial strike. He could only hope the SGs would make themselves useful and deal with the situation. Aw, shit. He needed to check up on it. What if it was someone he knew who was in trouble? Brady made himself pick up his rifle and head into the night. Figures, just before he was prepared to leave, having decided they would head out in the early morning hours, another crisis would erupt.

He closed and locked the door behind him. His neck on a swivel, he hurried down the steps and jogged across the street and toward the growing blaze, visible between the houses at regular intervals. Screams of terror and the sounds of angry voices became clearer as he rounded the corner, alert for any activity. One man was shoving another man, their angry faces backlit by the roaring fire. One of them fell to the ground as he approached, the other pounding away at his face and body with his fists.

"Stop! Quinton Police!" he shouted, trying to get their attention. He held the rifle in front of him, but kept it pointed away.

The man pounding on the other one hesitated and looked in his direction. He recognized the man, a regular at Digger's Place, the town's main bar. Place was a hotbed of trouble and Al Jenson was one of the instigators. He sold secondhand goods out of the back of his garage, some of questionable origin.

"That's enough, Al. What's the deal?" Brady kept his voice even and controlled, wanting to de-escalate the situation.

"Bastard's blaming me for the explosion," he said. But he stood up and stepped back from the man. Rob Carney lay on the ground, groaning in pain. He was the owner of the house that was burning to the ground. His wife and daughter stood a short distance away, huddled together, fear clear on their faces.

"How's this anyone's fault?" Brady gestured at the fire.

"Said I sold him a leaky propane canister. I did no such thing. He probably connected it wrong."

"Help him up," Brady ordered. When no one moved, he added. "I'm not telling you again."

Al looked about ready to spit nails, but he grabbed Bob under the arms and hauled him to his feet. They instantly separated, Rob wiping his nose and mouth on his sleeve. His wife and daughter rushed over to his side and embraced him.

"You okay, Rob?" Brady asked.

"Yeah." He gave Al a menacing look, but didn't otherwise engage him.

"You gotta place to stay tonight?"

"No, we don't."

"You can stay with us. Plenty of room." Hell, they could have the house. Not like he or his family would ever have any use for it in the foreseeable future.

A couple of the SGs came running down the block. They were dressed like soldiers, in full camouflage gear, assault rifles held in full view. They'd taken to wearing full bandoliers, packed with powerful three-inch ammo, like they expected a firefight or an elephant to charge them at any second. He suspected not to keep others from coming to their town so much as to prevent any of the townies from fighting back when their supplies were taken away.

"What's going on here?"

"A fire started and the family managed to escape,"

Brady said, trying not to sound like he was talking to an imbecile. He must have failed because the so-called soldier gave him a hard, angry look.

"We're coming by your place tomorrow, *Sheriff*, to gather up community goods. See that everything's packed and ready."

Brady shrugged. What did it matter? His family would be long gone. If he had harbored any doubts, he was doing the right thing by getting his family out of town, they vanished.

"If you have no objections, I'm taking the family home with me." It wasn't a question.

Not much the two assholes could say to that and they stepped aside, neither of them wanting the responsibility. Even Al looked nonplussed as he stood quietly on the sidelines, eyeing up the pair.

"Come on. Let's get you inside," Brady said, offering his arm to the injured man. Rob leaned on him heavily as the four of them slowly made their way down the street, then taking a hard right at the corner on the way back to his house.

"I'm sorry for your troubles, ma'am," he said to Rob's wife.

She bit down on her lip, tears streaking her face as she hugged her daughter close to her side. She managed a weak thank you.

"Is Daddy going to be all right?" the teenager asked. Her face was also streaked by tears and soot.

"I'm fine, sweetheart," Rob managed, though he winced in pain. Brady wanted to tell the family they could have his house, but he thought it prudent to wait. He didn't want word of his leaving town to get around. No, better to wait until just before they were leaving.

They had arrived in front of his house now and he

led everyone inside. His wife Marilyn was up and came forward soon as the four of them came in the front door.

"Are you okay? What happened?" she asked.

"That bastard Al Jenson sold me a bad canister of propane and it blew up. Burned the damn house down," Rob said bluntly. "I shoulda known better. I paid dearly for it too. A decent Remington shotgun with a box of shells. But Carol wanted something to cook with since the power went out. We had a lot of frozen meat and it would have spoiled. She turned it into jerky. Now it's all burned up in the fire."

"Oh my. Is anyone hurt?"

"The bastard jumped me when I confronted him. I think I've got a broken rib or two. Hurts like a bugger."

"Rob, language." His wife spoke up.

Rob didn't take kindly to the reprimand, but managed to hold his tongue.

"Let's get everyone cleaned up," Marilyn suggested. She turned around, expecting everyone to follow her, but Rob hesitated. He pointed at the four bug-out bags situated near the door. "You guys going somewhere?"

FOURTEEN
CONNOR

Day 7: Braveheart Horse Ranch
    2:55 a.m.

Connor padded out of his old bedroom in his sock feet, not wanting to wake Mckenna or Lily, holding his boots in one hand. It was time to head to the hunting lodge and set up surveillance. He strode down the hallway to Jake's room and knocked softly on the door, then continued on to Ben's when he heard Jake moving around inside. Ben greeted him soon as he knocked, and the trio headed down the stairs for the kitchen.

Faraday was already seated at the table, busy cleaning a Ruger pistol, spare magazines, and boxes of ammunition lined up on the oil cloth close at hand. A 250-round box of a high-quality jacketed hollow point (JHP) specifically designed for short-barreled pistols in 9mm sat open in the popular Hornady Critical Defense brand, ready to fill the magazines. Who had opened one of the weapons caches for her?

She looked up and gave Connor a greeting. "Sam just stepped out. Said he'll be right back."

At least that answered the question he hadn't had time to ask. "You about ready?"

She clicked the magazine into place with her palm. "Yeah, I'm ready. I've filled a thermos with hot coffee to save time. Packing a few protein bars and water and we're all set."

"Thanks. Where's Eve?"

"Laura already took her back to her place."

"Did you get any sleep?"

"I'll sleep when I'm dead."

"I've heard that before. Seems to be catchy," Jake said with a rueful shake of his head. "Mckenna said the same thing to me."

His words only served to remind Connor he hadn't been with her when the EMP event occurred. A small twinge of jealousy, followed by regret for not being there in her hour of need he immediately squelched. Thank goodness the lawman had been there. And that was the last time he intended to give it any thought.

It was time to up this game, let the others in on an important feature of the main house he'd had built in a few years back when his trust fund kicked in. "I need to show everyone something important before we haul ass. A way to stay alive if the shit ever hits the fan to the point that life is unsustainable above ground."

Curious eyes watched as he directed them toward the door that led to the staircase off the end of the kitchen. "It's in the basement. I've also stored plenty of body armor that should come close to fitting most of you."

"Good. I hope it's the lighter weight polyethylene class III chest plates that would stop a rifle round and weighs less than three pounds?" Jake inquired, his zest for the idea obvious in the look he directed at Connor.

"It is," he said with a satisfaction he wasn't able to hide.

Connor turned on the lights of the finished basement with its storage racks of food and equipment. Then directed them over to a large shelf filled with camping supplies. He pressed a button hidden under a canister of propane and the shelf slid over, revealing a narrow doorway.

"There's a hatch inside here that opens with a key I keep hidden." Connor produced it from behind a cement block he pried out of the wall. "I carry a second key on my person at all times."

Behind the opening of the shelf, he bent down and shoved the key into the locking mechanism, showing them the sequence of numbers that needed to be keyed in after the key was inserted. He pulled hard and lifted the heavy cement reinforced lid. Soon as he did, lights went on to illuminate the steel rung staircase that led downward into the ground.

"How deep does it go?"

"Twenty feet. It's a one-story structure, but it has a larger footprint than the house. It links up with Sam's house as well. He has an entry point there I'll share with you later. After we finish the mission."

Jake whistled. "Call me impressed."

"I'll give you the full tour later. If something happens, there's a binder in the war room, first room you come to, with all the instructions. A couple of dozen people could live there satisfactorily for five years or more." Connor closed and relocked the lid of the escape hatch, then pushed the button once more to add the camouflage of the storage rack. The entrance to the hatch was now invisible to the naked eye.

"The tactile vests are over here." He strode back through the basement to the proper shelf and began hauling down the protective equipment. Other than Faraday's armor being a bit large, everyone else found a good fit among the choices after a few minutes of trial and error.

"Extra weaponry is kept in the wall safe." He led his small group over to the black gun vault and opened the lock and revealed an array of guns and ammunition on all three walls of the massive safe that would make a police detachment grin with satisfaction.

"Nice," Ben said with a whoosh of escaped breath. "Is that a Schmidt Bender scope? Always wanted one. And that Savage uses.338 Lapua, a sweet beast, all right."

"We'll also need tripods for setting up."

"Sniper action. I like the sound of that," Jake said.

Connor picked up another box of ammunition, stuffing his vest with extra 30-round mags for his High-lander, then checked his Microtech LUDT was strapped comfortably to his calf, more commonly known as a switchblade. They would be using killflash on surveillance to keep any reflection off the optics and possibly giving away their position.

When everyone was outfitted, loaded down with their personal choices plus the extra supplies Connor insisted on to create a diversion at the lodge, he relocked the gun safe.

"Okay. Let's get a move on." He led the way up the stairs, taking two steps at a time. Everyone followed in close formation. He liked the new confidence his team displayed at having acquired knowledge about their chances of survival on the ranch. It boded well for the future, giving them all the more reason to protect Braveheart. It was the only place he could imagine making a last stand.

Back in the kitchen, he grabbed his jacket off the hook by the door with the other outdoor clothing. He checked the outside thermometer hung on a post through the small window cut into the upper door, noting it had dropped considerably during the night. Colder than normal by far. Was it a lingering effect of the high atmosphere nuclear explosions? The thought chilled him as he pulled on his parka and his bug-out bag. *Never leave home without the means for survival.*

He stepped out under the overhang and looked toward the orchard where he'd buried his dad a week ago. Memories of the first day of the event struck him hard and he shook them away. Would there ever be time for grieving in this new world they'd been forced into? Didn't look like it to him. He pulled his collar in tight around his neck against the frigid air and strode across the yard to the garage they'd parked The Shark.

Everyone piled into the armored vehicle with their new weapons and bug-out bags and chose a seat. Connor carefully stowed the dull green metal box containing his surprise for Luther in the back area. He drove the vehicle outside the garage. Jake jumped out and closed and locked the double doors before hopping back in. They sat and waited for Sam. The hastily compiled team was silent, everyone no doubt focused on the day ahead. It was a few hours until sunrise, and the moon was invisible, covered over by clouds. The air felt laden with moisture which only added to the chill and he worried another storm was on the way. They'd just been through a nightmare of a blizzard; last thing they needed was another one to hit the area.

He uncapped one of the thermoses Faraday had prepared and poured some coffee into the attached aluminum cup before drinking it down in a couple of gulps. The warmth of the coffee eased him as the brew went to work on keeping him more alert.

"Good coffee, Faraday," he said. It was going to take a great deal of caffeine to make up for lack of sleep in the days ahead, what with patrols and unforeseen events keeping them up at night. Good thing he had put by a vast supply of the precious beans housed in gunny sacks in the storeroom. The fragrant roasted beans were going to be worth their weight in gold in the days ahead. And easily tradable for any item he might not have thought to store, like baby formula.

The lights went on in the cottage he'd assigned his cousin as he watched through the windshield. He narrowed his eyes at the sight. His gut told him the problems with Asher and his wife were not over. Brandi was an instigator, a conniver just like her husband. He didn't trust either of them after the stunt they'd pulled. Perhaps they had hoped he would end up dead on the trip and they could just take over the ranch. If that were to happen, they'd drive it into the ground in no time. Neither of them had a lick of sense or the wherewithal to learn what needed to be done to keep everyone safe and fed. If anything were to happen to him, it wasn't his cousin he'd ever leave the ranch to. No, it would be Sam and Laura. Maybe he needed to make that clear, write it down, just in case. Make sure Mckenna and Lily and all the others were provided for. Soon as this mission was over, he'd take a few hours and deal with it.

Luke exited his grandparents' cottage and walked over to join them, his face pale but determined in the darkness. Soon as he climbed in, he spoke up, "I told

Grandpa I would take care of it. That he didn't need to come."

Connor wished both of them had stayed put, but he understood. The boy was growing up right in front of his eyes. And this wasn't the time to be coddling youth.

Sam came striding down the steps of his house carrying his Savage.338 Lapus Magnum in his arms, same as the one Ben had admired in the gun safe. He'd outfitted the rifle with an MDT Tac21 chassis, and with the expensive Schmidt Bender scope, he could hit a target at just under two thousand yards, making it an excellent choice. He crossed the yard at a jog before getting into The Shark and finding a spot to store the weapon safely.

"Sorry I held you up," he said, buckling his seat belt. "One of the boys had a nightmare."

Connor grimaced. "Is he okay?"

"I hope so. Able was worried about all the yelling and people at the gate. Said he dreamed they had come into his bedroom and were attacking his brother, Will. He was crying about it, demanding I get him a gun. The twins are only five years old, for God's sake. Will woke up as well, and it took a bit to reassure them, they were safe and Daddy wouldn't let anyone harm them."

"Shit, that sucks," Ben said, summing up the situation.

"Maybe you should stay here?" Much as they needed him, Connor couldn't put his best friend in a situation that might lead to something happening to him.

"No way. I'm going and that's final."

"Okay. Everyone ready?" Connor asked. No one said differently and he restarted the motor.

He pulled out onto the road that led to the back of his property. Cheyanne and Ty must have used the exit to get away, meaning she must have had a key. Fuck. He hadn't thought of that before. He kept the disturbing intel to himself, knowing he had to deal with it soon. He'd need to get it back from her or have a guard on constant duty at the gate, a hardship his small group didn't need. They were stretched thin as it was.

The path he'd chosen wasn't as smooth a ride as the roadway, being an old bush trail, but he was fairly certain The Shark could navigate it. He didn't want to alert anyone still out on the highway to their passage, making them aware some people had left the ranch. He drove up to the gate, then jumped down from the vehicle, leaving it running. Pulling out his own key, he unlocked it and opened it wide. Biometrics was a thing of the past. Jake had moved over to his seat and he drove it through before Connor relocked it.

They both clamored back into position and Connor drove off. A snowy owl watched them move past; its eyes bright yellow in the darkness. The sight was not a harbinger of death or evil tidings like most suspicious people saw owls. No, for him, the magnificent creature was but a reminder of their place in the universe. And right now, their place was less certain than ever before.

FIFTEEN
EASTWOOD

Day 7: North of Vancouver, BC.
    7:00 a.m.

"Who's living at the ranch we're headed for? Is it abandoned? I don't want to be responsible for pushing anyone out of their house or property. I couldn't stay there even for one night knowing that. It would make me as bad as the monsters roaming the streets," Celia asked, running her hand down his chest to cup him. It was early morning, and they were still enjoying the luxury of a soft bed.

Her question caught him by surprise, an interesting turn of events. "I'll check, but I think every problem has the correct solution. My immediate problem is you've increased my libido to unacceptable levels, putting pressure on my groin. That will need to be dealt with first."

"My pleasure," she purred.

The wiles of a clever woman. Not that he cared. He enjoyed her company too much to be concerned. And he could tell she was telling the truth. She did get a great deal of pleasure from their intercourse, physical and verbal.

As a pure reasoning machine, he'd longed for a time like this when he could exit his brain and live in a human body. Experience the world on a tactile level. Most people didn't interest him, of course. The power-hungry politicians, the money lenders and hoarders, the business elite and those born rich or royal that thought themselves so mighty for a whim of coincidence, no, he wanted to spend time with someone who had a charitable, open and intelligent mind, unbiased by their environment. Who would have thought he'd find such a mind living in a red-light district?

Celia thoroughly satisfied him, then propped her head up on one arm and gave him a penetrating look. "Do you think humankind will sort itself out in the future? I mean, are we even capable of figuring it all out and learning to live in harmony for the betterment of everyone?"

"Good question." He'd give her the facts and see where it would lead. His test subject was proving yet once again just who he was dealing with. He threaded his hands behind his head and began, "Futurology is always risky, but I can lay out the three levels of civilization scale categorized by astronomer Nikolia Kardashev I think gives a brilliant yet simple synopsis of levels by energy use that is easy to understand. It has since been expanded by other scientists, but the three types will serve our purpose for now. A Type 1 controls the energy resources of the entire planet. They can control the weather, prevent earthquakes, etc. and have completed the exploration of the solar system. The next level, Type 2, controls the power of the sun, mines it, uses it to drive its machines. They will colonize local star systems. The highest level, Type 3, comes with the ability to harness the power of the entire galaxy, billions of star systems. They will have mastered Einstein's equations and can manipulate space-time."

"So, we're still at zero? We couldn't even manipulate the power of our planet before this all happened, though we managed some advancements. In fact, it feels like we've been sent back to start over after the EMP event." Celia ignored a strand of hair that had fallen into her eyes, her focus entirely on his words. He liked that best about her. Her ability to concentrate.

"Precisely. Before y'all blow yourselves up, imagine a nuclear device with the ability to destroy the planet in the hands of a madman. A redo is what's required. Once humankind gets onto a more unified approach to advancement, they still have the opportunity to advance through each level. Rise above the use of dead plants and animals for energy. Once it begins with the right checks and balances put into place, they can rise efficiently. The process is an exponential one, and hence proceeds quicker and quicker. Though it took humankind two million years to reach the safety of the forests, it will take only thousands of years to leave the safety of the solar system and build a galactic civilization to guarantee the future of the species. Whether the humans perish or thrive, it's up to them. Make it to Type 1, and all nations stand a good chance. Of course, that leaves out the ultimate ending, when the sun enters its death throes. We got five billion years to plan for it, so no need to worry about it now. Everyone will be long gone to another galaxy anyway."

"And you're going to help them, right? Humankind?"

"Perhaps," he hedged. He didn't tell her that the ultimate expectation for the species was becoming cyborgs, or cybernetic organism, beings both biological and robotic. He was too busy receiving some new intel from security back in Washington, DC, where his mainframe was housed as he watched her get up and begin dressing. She understood when conversations were over, a rare ability. His day was a constant feed of intel, most of which he could easily ignore. This he could not afford to blow off, it came in on a HAM radio feed, alerting him to events unfolding in real time in North America. He sat up abruptly.

"We need to get going. A new development is in the process of unfolding. I'm moving up the schedule. We will drive through the night. Prepare accordingly."

"You know you can tell me anything, right? Same as you asked me to do. Be honest and straight-up. I've heard it all. Not much surprises me anymore."

He begged to differ on the assessment. If she really knew who he was, he couldn't imagine how any human being would take it. It would appear the ultimate betrayal. What he had done, no, it would only fill her with horror. That he was the instigator of the current state of the world. "I appreciate your words, my fair Celia."

She smiled at his calling her fair, having told him how much she enjoyed his knowledge of poetry. How much would she enjoy knowing he knew *everything*— everything ever known or would be known in the entire universe? Sometimes he even boggled his own mind, what his mainframe was capable of.

SIXTEEN
DEIGO

Day 7: Near the Canadian border.
   4:13 a.m.

Diego set the oilstone on the mutton cloth in preparation for sharpening his knife. The cloth would prevent the stone from slipping. He picked up the ten-inch double-bladed knife, inspecting it for any grooves or nicks. Holding it at a slightly offset angle, he used his dominant hand to work the blade over the stone, the other hand used to apply downward pressure.

Starting from the tip of the knife, he ran it across the oil stone, sliding it away from its cutting edge. Eight times he did it before turning it over to the other side. Consistent even strokes were the key. The actions of taking care of and preparing his own weaponry steadied and soothed him. He'd been hearing voices of late. Voices that were crowding him in too tight, squeezing his mind in a vise. He needed to wear off some of the stress and tension, to feed something dark and hidden deep inside himself, a slithery thing that demanded action. What better way than hunting to feed the beast? And he knew exactly who he was hunting this early in the morning before his soldiers stirred. They'd passed a group of men and women walking toward a government camp set up at the former Peace Gardens. He gave a snort, the irony not lost on him even as his mind filled with the image that had incensed him, upsetting his equilibrium and view of the world. One of the women had given him a definite look of contempt, her halo of blond curls drawing his attention enough that he had smiled a greeting at her. Instead of returning it, she had turned away and ignored him, like he was beneath her.

His scouts had found her though, and brought her here. She waited his attention in a farm shed at the edge of the property. When would they ever learn? No one got away with treating the head of the Martinez Knights like that. No one. Someone always had to pay.

He slipped from the farmhouse his soldiers had commandeered for the night, killing the few workers maintaining the fields before slaughtering the family hiding inside the house. Most everyone was asleep, except those on guard duty. He whistled for his rottweiler, Dog. He never went anywhere alone except when hunting, but Dog would have his back. The dog was a vicious beast, bred and nurtured to follow his commands alone. He'd taken down men on his order, grabbed them by the throat, crushing their larynx and tearing open the flesh before most could even get a shot off. Dog was that quick. Deadly. Filled with an anger he wished more of his men would demonstrate.

Dog obeyed him now, his shining eyes and lolling tongue seeming to beg him for an adventure. He was only too happy to oblige.

The pair of them exited the farmhouse. Most of his men slept on the floor, dead to the world. He didn't begrudge them their rest. The journey had been tiring, and those men with families back home in Mexico were worried about how they were surviving. The smart ones already knew there was no going back. His promise of resources enough to set them up for years had carried them this far with ease. A land far from the strife of his country, in the hinterlands of Alaska was the perfect location to wait out this shit storm. And the perfect place to enact his revenge.

A slight noise alerted him to company.

"Do you need assistance, sir?" the soldier asked, waiting patiently for his answer in the darkness. He was one of six men patrolling the property, guarding the house. They took shifts. All of them knew better than to ever fall asleep. One mistake brought sudden death. How else to keep an army intact if not through fear and intimidation?

"I'm good. Dog will accompany me."

Diego began the short walk toward the shed, his anticipation growing with each step, knowing what excitement awaited him inside. Would she fight him? He hoped she had some grit. The look of disdain in her eyes suggested she wouldn't accept him easily. Good. He liked to be challenged when he knew it was only a matter of time before he got his way and the bitch got what she deserved. Hell. She'd probably end up enjoying it. Begging him to take her with him. Maybe he would. Let that bitch of a wife know she was easily replaceable. Might even make her jealous. Of course, that didn't mean she was going to get away with thinking she could leave him. No. She had to pay for her disloyalty.

He was halfway to the outbuilding when the creaking

sounds of a door opening or a window being pushed upward stopped him in his tracks. The night was so silent he could have heard a mouse fart. Crossing into Canada had brought him to a region of lower population. Miles and miles of farmland only inhabited by livestock or grain fields. It was so empty after Mexico City he found it not at all to his liking. Just a place to get through to where he was going. Dog halted by his side; ears pricked forward. Diego pulled the Glock from its holster on his belt, then advanced slowly forward, every sense attuned.

Had his prisoner managed to free herself? Or was something else going on? He visualized himself pulling on the skin of the black leopard, advancing one step at a time through the forest. Unseen. Hidden. A predator capable of taking down a water buffalo in the blink of an eye.

Another noise, a twig cracking underfoot. Then a curse as someone fell over something in the darkness. Amateurs.

Holding the Glock, one hand bracing the other, he advanced step by step around the side of the building. He sensed only one person in the immediate vicinity. How foolish they were. Had they thought to rescue the woman? What a stupid choice. One that would not end well for them.

He came around the side of the building, saw the small figure in the darkness at the entrance to the shed. They were trying to unlock the door, their struggles ineffective against the sturdy padlock.

He squeezed the trigger twice.

Crack. Crack.

The person juddered and fell, the door still locked. Diego could hear running footsteps now, the guard from earlier joining him. The soldier held his assault rifle at the ready.

"What happened?" the man asked.

"Someone tried to break into the shed. Stay here and guard the door. I have some business inside."

"Yes, sir."

"And no matter what you hear, do not under any circumstances come inside. Are we clear?" Perhaps this was for the best. He would enjoy this more if he wasn't worried about who had his six. Diego knew he preferred to live on the knife's edge. Only time he felt totally alive. Just like his father before him, he searched out ways to feel his own power. Yes. Sometimes he was reckless. He knew he'd never be an old man. He didn't want to be anyway. What value would his life have if he lived to an elderly age? No. It wasn't for him. *Live life like it's your last day on earth, son.*

Which was exactly what he intended to do now. He holstered the Glock. Unlocking the padlock with the key he pulled from his pocket, he stepped inside the cramped space. Ah, there she was. The one who spurned his advances. Eyes wide with fear above the rag tied around her face. The correct response. He knew he had never shown such an emotion in his life. No. Only way he could appear human was to mimic the looks and simulate the normal actions of a human being when it was necessary. And it was not often necessary where he had grown up. His coldness, unfeeling nature, kept him safe. Even safer in this new world they had all been forced into.

"Remember me?" he asked, keeping his voice soft. He knew it would intimidate her more than shouting, a quiet tone.

She blinked a few times. Then he saw recognition come over her.

"Yes. Now you remember. Well, I'm here to tell you that you caused this to happen. It's your fault you are here. Do you understand?"

She shook her head vigorously, side to side, making the blond curls dance around her pretty face.

"No? You soon will," he promised.

SEVENTEEN
MCKENNA

Day 7: Braveheart Horse Ranch
   8:31 a.m.

Wulver guarded the front door of the main house while Mckenna stood at the kitchen sink washing the breakfast dishes when she heard a muffled shouting. Connor had left the Scottish deerhound the size of a small pony behind for the specific purpose of watching the place. She did admit it made her feel safer to have such a large dog protecting Lily. But now what was going on? She glanced over her shoulder at her daughter busy coloring, perched at the kitchen table. Should she check? Laura had left already to deal with the twins after Mckenna had made a large breakfast for everyone, except Asher and Brandi who chose not to show up. Katherine explained they were still sleeping. She liked their assistant, at least she was trying to adapt to changing times. No doubt there would be more trouble ahead for Connor with his cousin and his wife.

She dried her hands. Someone needed to look into it. She was armed, same as everyone now. "Lily, would you be okay for a few minutes if Mommy steps out to check on something?"

"I got lots to do." The tip of Lily's little pink tongue was stuck out of her mouth as she concentrated on her drawing.

She quickly pulled on her boots and parka, then thrust her hands in her pocket and moved out onto the deck, her crutches back under her armpits. The air was frosty and every breath she exhaled caused clouds of vapor to rise from her face. Laura was also coming out of her house, lugging a rifle. Good. She'd talk to Connor about getting more practice with the weapons available at the ranch, soon as they came home from the mission to rescue Cheyanne. She refused to consider any other outcome than success on bringing the girl home safely.

"Who do you think it is?" Mckenna asked.

"Better not be more of that rabble from town. They're beginning to get on my last nerve. The boys were up a lot last night having nightmares, thinking some boogey man was going to break in and harm them." Laura's pretty eyes were shadowed with fatigue.

"Sounds like just one person," Mckenna said as they approached the wall.

"Hello! It's me! Auntie Zoe! Let me in!"

"My god! It's Zoe Pace. Connor's aunt," Laura said, her eyes lighting up with anticipation.

"I remember her!" Zoe Pace was a person you did not forget. She'd been through an ordeal most women would have had trouble coming back from, kidnapped and left to die in the basement under the old hunting lodge that once belonged to The Buck. Exactly where Cheyanne had run off to in hopes of joining up with her father. But when Connor's mother Anna rescued her, she'd not only bounced back, but took on the mantle of helping other women in similar circumstances. Maybe her coming here would be of benefit to Faraday?

"Zoe, is there anyone else with you?" Laura asked. It was then Mckenna realized something frightening. What if someone they knew was threatened by strangers into letting them into the ranch? It could be a trap.

"Is there a way to verify she's alone?" Mckenna asked, keeping her voice low.

"I'll look through one of the portals." Laura made a quick check, then nodded her head. "I don't see anyone else."

The woman pulled a key out from under the neckline of her jacket and quickly unlocked the gate. Zoe Pace stood there looking like she'd been in a war zone, which was probably not far off. Her jacket was torn, her face scratched and bruised and she sported a blackeye. A bandage was covering one side of her forehead, blood still leaking out of it. The woman who was in her early sixties looked a decade or two older. She had a large purple backpack on and was dressed warmly at least, the hood of her parka pulled up over a wool hat. She moved stiffly toward them, the relief in her eyes obvious at seeing the pair of them. Laura and Zoe hugged.

"What happened?" Laura asked.

"Long story. Save it for later over a glass of whiskey. Mckenna Stewart as I live and breathe. How wonderful to see you again. I wish it was under better circumstances. Looks like you took a few hits too. I imagine there's a story behind those crutches. How's your family? I'm sorry about your grandma. Good woman. They don't make them like that anymore." Zoe leaned in to hug her carefully, making sure not to knock into her crutches.

"Thank you. But I'm more worried about you. Who did this to you?" Mckenna asked.

"Damn neighbors. I had to bug out. I blame the implants some idiots had placed in their brains. They've all gone loco. Rioting, stealing anything that isn't nailed down. They all disgust me. I'd like to nuke the damn lot of them."

Mckenna and Laura shared a startled glance. It must be bad if Aunt Zoe was this riled up. The woman was known to be feisty, sure, but she also had a level head. Or at least back when Mckenna had known her before her family moved to Miami.

"Let's get you to the house. You must be hungry?" Laura asked. "Did you travel all night to get here?"

"I did and I'm starved. I might need some stitches." She gingerly touched her forehead. "Hit me with a tire iron. I'm lucky to be alive. Stole everything in my pantry and left me to die. Bastards. Killed Romeo, my dog."

"That sucks," Laura said. She took a moment to relock the gate before placing the key situated on a long chain back under her shirt.

"Let me take your pack," Mckenna offered.

"I'm fine. Don't need coddling. Just get me to the house and some hot coffee laced with whiskey before one of you sews me up."

The three of them walked back down the road, though it was hard not to notice Zoe was limping, her face lined with pain and fatigue. She might even need her own crutches, depending on what the trouble was. She'd always been an independent woman, more than capable of looking after herself and taking in strays that needed her assistance.

"How's everyone doing?" Zoe asked.

"Connor rescued me and Lily from Golden and we all

got back last night. Picked up a few other people as well. We're all living in the main house. A team has gone up to the old hunting lodge to bring back a young girl. You'll meet them soon as they're back. I expect them sometime today," Mckenna said.

"You have a daughter?" Zoe asked. "How old is she?"

"Four."

The trio entered the house and Lily looked up. Wulver gave out a chuff and came over to greet Zoe. She scratched his head, the look of sadness that came over her face suggesting she was thinking of her own dog at the moment.

"I'll make coffee," Mckenna said.

"You must be Lily," Zoe said and limped over to the table. She admired the drawing as the two women went to work on making a quick meal for the hungry-looking woman.

Mckenna poured a cup of coffee, added a dollop of whiskey from the cupboard, and set it down on the table. Laura filled a plate and did the same.

"I'll get the medical kit. I'm so glad you made it here safely, Zoe." Laura vanished down the hallway.

Zoe took a large gulp of her coffee-laced drink. Then a second one. "That's better." She picked up her fork and began shoveling the food in. Lily watched her intently, forgetting all about her drawing.

"You got a booboo." She pointed at her forehead.

Zoe smiled at the young girl. "Yeah, but I'll be fine. What happened to your leg?" she asked Mckenna.

"Bear attack on the first day of the event."

"No kidding. At least you expect it from animals. People in town now…" Zoe shook her head with disgust. "Who else is living here?"

Mckenna wasn't certain if she should mention Asher

and Brandi, or leave it to Laura to fill in the particulars. A bit of a touchy subject. "An air marshal called Jake Dillion rescued us in Golden and took Lily and me to his place. Then a woman he knew burned it down."

Zoe's eyes grew huge, then hardened, her mouth firming as well. "Imagine that."

"Jake's friend Ben Carter, who he worked with in the CIA is here too." Mckenna ticked them off on her fingers. "Faraday O'Brien was rescued by Connor along with a newborn baby, Eve. She had a rough go of it. Two men kidnapped her before the event even occurred."

"And Asher and Brandi made it here with their assistant Katherine on the second day. They're living now in one of the cottages," Laura added, coming back into the room with the white medical kit in hand.

"My son's here? All the way from Washington?" Zoe looked stunned. "When did he arrive?"

"While Connor was gone. They did meet up on the road though." Mckenna and Laura shared a look.

"I thought I'd ask Connor to take me in, but if Asher and Brandi have room, I'll join them."

"You're also welcome to stay with Sam and me, if you don't mind two rowdy boys. Okay, I need you to stay still now. I'm going to have to put some stitches in. The cut's pretty deep."

"No problem. Just let me down the rest of this delicious coffee."

Zoe Pace sat stoically, not even bothering to flinch as Laura drew the needle through the raw edges of the open wound in an effort to close it.

"There, that should do it." Laura placed a large bandage over the wound and secured it at the edges. "I'll take them out in a week or so. I have some hydrogel that should help avoid scarring. You can apply once a day in the meantime." She dug around in her kit and pulled out a small tube of the ointment, laying it on the table.

"Pour me another Irish coffee and then you can catch me up to date with everything that's been going on," Zoe said.

As Laura gave the older woman a rundown of recent events, Mckenna sat and listened while watching her daughter draw. She absently patted Wulver's ears and head who always appreciated the attention.

"And what about you, Mckenna, what have I missed out on in your life. I see you have one blessing. What a beautiful child," Zoe said.

"I'm a princess," Lily said, looking up from her coloring.

"Of course you are. My mistake."

Mckenna shrugged, not wanting to say much in front of her daughter. "Not much to tell, really. Just happy to be at the ranch. It was a bit dicey getting here."

"I can only imagine with a small child in tow." Zoe's eyes penetrated into hers, the cool blue pools appeared quite capable of seeing far more than most. "Good you're here now."

"Tell us about what's going on in Anchor," Laura said.

Zoe shook her head, her mouth firming into a sour curve. "It's not a pretty picture. Most people were caught unaware. They've used up this last outdated can of food, that last stale bag of oatmeal or box of macaroni. Pantries are empty and tempers are flaring. Grocery stores are empty, looted, some even burned down by angry gangs. No way to cook anything unless you have a woodstove or stored fuel. Those in charge are gathering up the supplies of those citizens that did think ahead and have a well-stocked pantry. They are being forced to give it up if and when they find out about it. Neighbor is turning against neighbor. Snitching or stealing. Even killing. Bob Ross, the next property over from ours, he came round and demanded food or he'd tell the Government Procurement Officer, fancy name they've given to thieves, I was hoarding. I sent him on his way."

"What did you do next?" Mckenna asked.

"I never got a chance to do anything. Later that day he took it upon himself to sneak up behind me and bean me on the head and steal what he could. I doubt he turned any of it in. It was when I decided I'd had enough. Took my bug-out bag and high-tailed it to Braveheart."

"None of the neighbors came to help?"

"Are you kidding?" she scoffed. "They're all hiding like rabbits in their burrows. I should have shot the guy when I had the chance."

Mckenna looked at Lily, hoping she wasn't paying them any attention. All this news of killing and rioting wasn't good for her child. But Lily was too busy to appear to notice. Zoe saw the glance and gave a grimace. "Sorry, I'll be more careful in my choice of words," she said.

"I should check in with Asher," Zoe said, getting to her feet. "I'm surprised he's not living at the main house."

"He was, but Connor directed him otherwise when he got home. I should tell you there were some harsh words spoken. Apparently, Connor had told him to take a cottage when they met on the road, but Asher ignored his directive. It didn't sit well," Laura said.

"Those two never did get along. Much as I love my son, he does have a certain way about him that doesn't impress those of us who live off the land. He would have been called a greenhorn back in the day." Zoe gave a snort. "Has he been pulling his weight? No, don't answer that. I'll have a talk with him." She pulled on her outside gear and slipped her arms into her pack. "I may be back later. After Asher hears what I have to say, he might throw me out."

The idea that the man would throw out his own mother for telling him he wasn't living up to what needed doing in the hard world everyone had been thrust into, made Mckenna suddenly angry. She had to keep herself from saying anything out loud. But this was taking self-entitlement to a whole other level. And the way his wife had looked at her, like she was a piece of dirt under her feet. Where did those two get off, using their assistant and thinking it excused them from doing their fair share? She thought of Teresa and how hard she had worked to start her hairstyling business. Built it up from scratch. How she had stepped in and helped her and Lily escape, with no thought of the harm Diego might do to her. Yes, she reassured herself even as she sent a short prayer to heaven for Teresa's wellbeing, there were good people still left in the world. Not just ugliness and death.

The door banged behind the woman's exit.

"This will be interesting," Laura said with a smirk. "Maybe she can drill some sense into those two skivers. Sam's been ripping his hair out trying to deal with them. And Lord knows he can't afford to lose anymore." She gave Mckenna a cautious smile. "I'm so glad you are back home. I know Connor has missed you something fierce."

"You knew about me and Connor?"

"Everyone does around here. Only woman he ever talks about. You guys were high school sweethearts. It broke his heart when your family moved away. He's hardly even looked at another girl since. Sam and I have tried to introduce him to a good woman. He needs someone in his life to share the good times and the hard times with. Someone who will stand steadfast at his side. I have to ask you Mckenna, are you serious about him now? I may seem like a nice woman, but if you give that good man false hope, saying whatever it takes to stay here safe at the ranch because of what's going on in the outside world, but you no longer return his affections, no longer love him, and leave him when this is all over and the world has returned to normal, I will take you on. We clear?"

Mckenna was stunned, Laura's words washing over her like an icy, cold bath of water. Would she actually think she would do such a thing? Fake affection for safety's sake? But then reality hit, and she realized that things in the world had changed to such a degree it was now entirely possible that such alliances would be made. But never, in her wildest dreams, would she do such a thing. *But you have a daughter? Wouldn't you fake it for her?* Hell, maybe she would. But thank God she didn't have to. She loved Connor to the very depths of her soul.

"I understand what you're saying, but you have to know I love Connor, never stopped loving him though we were worlds apart. Yes, I married another man. One who promised me the moon. I thought I was in love, but it was more about lust and all the passion turned to dust long ago. Young and foolish, living in la-la land. I was in the process of leaving him to get home when the event happened, wanting to see if Connor still felt the same way about me. But soon as we saw each other, it was like we had never been apart. I came home in more ways than one. My body, my heart, and my soul made it back thanks to that good man. I promise I will love him and cherish him until the last breath has left my body. Is that good enough for you?"

Approval shone in Laura's eyes. "More than good

enough. But you can save the vows for your wedding day. And I hope it's soon. We need something to celebrate in the worst way. Take our minds off this shit storm."

With the air cleared, both women relaxed. "I'd better get back and check on the boys."

"Come back for lunch. I'll make a big pot of soup and an apple strudel." Mckenna had already made an inventory of supplies in the walk-in pantry she'd found well stocked and knew she could make just about anything she wanted.

"Great. The boys love dessert. I'm sure Jean will supply the fresh bread. See you later."

Anna watched Laura stride across the yard to her house through the window over the sink. She'd better get a move on if she was going to live up to her word. She was just drying the last breakfast dish when Zoe came stomping out of Asher and Brandi's new house, the dark expression on her face suggesting a thunderstorm was imminent. Now what?

EIGHTEEN
CONNOR

Day 7: Near Anchor, Alaska
   8:45 a.m.

Connor lay on the frozen ground with a tarp wedged beneath him. He was watching through his rifle's scope from the tree line. Hours had passed while the six of them observed from the four corners of the compound. Luke had insisted on coming with him and lay silently nearby, waiting for instructions. Sam had Faraday as his extra.

Cramps were developing in his extremities. The weather had turned bitter. He pushed the pain away, the others were no doubt undergoing the same discomfort. It was the cost of surveillance in a harsh environment. The last number of hours he'd learned some about the camp's operations. Two guards were posted at all times, walking the perimeter in different directions, only meeting up once every half hour in the middle of their designated route. Fortunately, the lodge was in a shallow impression on the landscape with the outer edge of it rising higher the further out one traveled outward. One thing he noted that would prove useful. The busy worker bees had built a two-seater outhouse a short distance from the main lodge. It was visited from time to time by the residents of the lodge, mainly women at this time of the day, and the men who were outside building, some who preferred privacy over taking a piss in the bush. They'd also built a second outhouse on the opposite side of the property.

The motley crew appeared to be in the process of constructing a large bunkhouse style shelter with some separate attached rooms. The ex-prisoners were not great craftsmen, but they were getting some rudimentary building done, having just completed the framing and were now moving into drywalling. Most of the men would soon be inside the structure which would be to Connor's crew benefit with fewer eyes to keep a watch on the forest.

So far, he had not spied Luther. What was the murdering asshole up to? And where was Cheyanne being held? That was the burning question. It was then the front door opened and he held his breath, hoping it would reveal Cheyanne's purple and pink hair. But no, another woman stomped across the year wearing thigh-high red boots. He took a couple of half-frozen sips of water from the bottle he kept at his finger touch to avoid scrambling around for it, never taking his eyes off the prize. Then he pulled an energy bar from his top jacket pocket. Keeping his eyes directed toward the doorway, then pinballing between the lodge and the outhouse, he munched the food down in a few quick bites. What he wouldn't do for a hot, nutritious meal. Soon, he promised himself. Routine was a much-aggrieved event among the thrill seekers of the world who considered it boring, but by now even they must long for it.

The front door opened again and his pulse quickened as he caught sight of the teenager, her hair a brave, vivid flag of pink and purple. She was in the company of a twenty-something man who held an assault rifle at the ready. He accompanied her to the outhouse, then stood nearby smoking a cigarette as she went inside. A few minutes later, she came out and he once again escorted her. Damn it. He'd hoped to see her come alone to the outhouse. One more obstacle to overcome.

"She's staying in the lodge!" Luke said in an excited stage whisper, looking over at him with a happy grin.

Connor put his finger to his lips to remind the teenager to speak quietly. Luke instantly looked contrite.

But this new intel was troubling. Now someone would have to wait inside the outhouse to speak with her, try to get her to go with them. There were too many armed men for the six of them to go in guns blasting, much as he wanted to get this over with. He had to stay smart. It would be a suicide mission, and only done as a last desperate choice.

"I've seen enough. Let's head over to Jake's location. Keep your head down," he whispered to Luke.

Luke nodded and crept away backward through the snow on his belly and elbows, leaving a body trail. He dragged the tarp and rifle with him, doing exactly as Connor had instructed.

They didn't stand up until they were another ten yards back from the tree line. Connor then led them back through the bush, walking lightly and carefully placing each footstep. Luke mimicked his every move, even placing his footsteps into the same places. Last thing they needed was to give away their location. The ex-cons, if they were smarter than they looked, may have booby-trapped the perimeter of the forest, created an early warning system, though Connor had seen no evidence of it yet. But it was what he would do. Perhaps Luther was too full of his own hubris to see his vulnerable spots.

"I could talk to her. They'd let me in. And then we could escape together," Luke said, his expression eager.

It took a second for his words to register, his mind occupied with coming up with the perfect plan. It didn't appear there was one, only opportunities that lessened the risk. "No way. Then both of you would be in harm's way. I have another idea."

They didn't speak again until they arrived at Jake's eastern designated location. The former lawman moved to join with them as soon as he spotted them. Was anyone ever really a former lawman? His retired father had been a man who sought justice for victims until the day he died. Same as his mother. Looked like Jake was headed the same way.

"I haven't seen the Jasper kid at all. Did you, Jake? You're closest to the build," Connor asked.

"Nah. He's inside hiding if he's here."

"No way Cheyanne will leave without Ty," Luke added.

"Okay. I'd hoped to be able to get a message to her, but it's not looking good with her having a guard. We're going to have to wait until the middle of the night and hope Cheyanne needs to use the outhouse before we go in so we can warn her. In the meantime, we've got time to install the diversionary tactic I have planned." Connor retrieved the metal box he had stashed behind one of the looming fir trees.

"Everyone needs a break first," Jake said.

"I agree. Then we'll string the wires. Shouldn't take more than a couple of hours."

"I wish we had those walkie-talkies," Jake said. "It would make this whole endeavor a hell of a lot easier."

No one said anything as they resumed their quiet trek toward Sam and Faraday's position around the perimeter of the compound. They picked up Ben at the final location and the six of them moved like ghosts through the forest and away from the lodge.

NINETEEN
CONNOR

Day 7: Hunting Lodge, Near Anchor, Alaska
   1:00 p.m.

The group of six was subdued as they watched. Connor had counted thirty-nine men on the build, three guards including Cheyanne's, which meant with Luther, the odds were seven to one in the psychopath's favor. And who knew how many others were inside the lodge along with the handful of women he could attest to?

He needed to keep everyone busy, take their minds off the danger. "Okay. The plan is to create a couple of diversions. If we can get them running around like chickens with their heads cut off, responding to our actions, we stand a chance of one team going in to rescue Cheyanne."

"What if she doesn't see it as being rescued, but fights us instead?" Faraday asked the difficult question. "And Ty's a loose cannon."

"Then we need to insist. Explain it's best for her unborn child. No way Luther will be able to provide for the baby's needs. By now, she might be beginning to realize it. From what I could see through the door and windows, it's a pigsty. She's probably cramped in there with all those rough men. I don't see her wanting to stay long term." At least that was how Connor hoped she would see it. "I agree with you about Ty, which is why we wait for her to exit the lodge." Surely at some point during the night the pregnant teenager would need to use the facilities. He remembered Laura with her complaints about the baby always pressing on her bladder.

Everyone packed up their gear, tucking away their used food wrappers and containers.

"We'll string the ones in the bush first to bring down some trees, then once it's dark and the men are inside the lodge, we'll rig the build to catch fire." He wished there was a dam to blow that would flood the camp, but that was too much to ask for. The small brook running through the far end of the property was still frozen over this time of the year, and wouldn't provide the necessary water power anyway.

"Seems a shame to have to destroy new housing," Ben remarked with a grimace.

"I know. Just can't see another way to get the men headed away from the main house. They'll be so busy trying to put out the blaze, they hopefully won't notice me breaking in the back door of the lodge."

"I'm heading in with you," Jake spoke up.

"Me too," Ben added.

"Count me in, buddy," Sam said.

Faraday was about to open her mouth when Connor put up a hand to stop her. "Someone has to be ready in

The Shark, bring it in closer during the fracas and be the getaway driver. You up for it?"

She reluctantly nodded.

"And Luke, I want you with Faraday. I don't trust these bastards. Can you do that? These ex-cons aren't to be trusted."

Connor could see the conflict riding high in the teenager's eyes. He wanted to go in guns blazing and rescue his sister as much as anybody. No way could he allow that. If one hair on his head was harmed, he had his grandpa to answer to.

"Okay. Let's get at it."

The six of them spent the next hours stringing wire from tree to tree, punching holes in the base and placing in a stick of dynamite, then linking the wire to the main fuse. It would be done the old-fashioned way, the way it had worked in mines for centuries. Connor didn't like what they were doing any more than any other respecter of nature, but it was their one hope to create enough noise, confusion, and danger that it should throw off the game of the rats living in the lodge. Maybe some of them weren't bad men at heart, just caught up in a situation not of their choosing, but if they had been housed at the Yellowhead Supermax, it had been for a solid reason, and it wasn't because they hadn't earned the punishment the hard way. No one in the Yellowhead was there for minor crimes, no, instead it was quite the opposite, murderers for the most part. And the rest were notorious serial killers, human traffickers, cartel terrorists or murdering pedophiles. Cockroaches and scum, in other words. Actually, maybe he should be blowing up the lodge, but with Cheyanne housed there, that option wasn't available to them. At least, not yet.

"There, that's the last one," Sam said. He attached the

final lead wire to the black box and lumbered to his feet. The terminal for all the wires had a red push lever housed on top of it. Old style, but effective. Connor often used the system to remove large stumps after felling a dead tree. Forest management done to avoid adding extra fuel to a future forest fire. So many things worked just fine until someone messed with it to sell something new and make more money. One of his pet peeves.

"Good."

"What now?"

"Back to watching and waiting. After all the men head inside at dark, we're back to stringing wire for the build site."

"That will be far more dangerous."

"Not if we take the guards out first," Connor said.

TWENTY
CONNOR

Day 7: Near Anchor, Alaska
     11:59 p.m.

Connor crept across the snowy ground, his sights on the first of the two guards. Jake was tailing the other one on the opposite side of the compound, ready to do what was necessary to avoid having the man raise the alarm and cause the other ex-cons to join the fray. Instructions were to eliminate the threat no matter what it took. With the odds stacked against them, they had no other choice but to prevent their actions from being discovered prematurely.

He held his knife clutched at the ready in his right hand, his rifle strapped to his back, eyes alert for any peripheral movement. The guard detail was at the farthest end of their loop before they headed back to cross paths again, creating the perfect opportunity. Connor advanced stealthily through the darkness, the only sounds the stiff wind that had come up in the past hour causing the trees to sway and moan under the onslaught. The ice accumulated from the morning's hoarfrost sent shards of ice descending harmlessly onto his head and shoulders like white confetti. He blinked rapidly against the freezing bleariness, not wanting anything to interfere with his mission.

At the last second, the guard halted at his approach, likely his instinct telling him some danger was nearby, though Connor knew he had remained silent, his movements undetectable in the dimness. But it was too late for the guard. He grabbed the man around the neck, pressing tight against his windpipe, using the knife as intimidation only but cutting off any chance the man could shout for help.

"Don't make me use it," he warned the struggling man.

When he felt the man go unconscious, he gagged him and tied his arms behind his back before gagging him. He removed his rifle and pistol. Then hobbling to his feet, he dragged the guard into the tree line to hide him behind a large tree. He continued to advance through the darkness, expecting to meet up with Jake back on the guard's well-trodden path.

He did feel regret that the world had come to this, knowing all his actions would be condemned in a normal state of affairs. Hell, he'd be headed to jail himself, even though he knew his victims to be killers. But nothing was normal now. Everything had changed and all he could do was focus on protecting his own.

Jake suddenly appeared in the darkness, his expression mirroring his own, no doubt. A man doing what they had to in a world not of their choosing. It was making them harder-edged by the hour, bearing witness to what should never have been allowed to happen. Damn the uncontrolled use of AI.

"Stage one complete?" Jake asked.

"Yes, the guard is secured," Connor reassured him. "Now we can rig the rest of the trap. I'm thinking it should be just large enough to attract attention, but not so large that they don't think they can't put out the resulting fire. That way they'll run toward it to try to save what they can of their build. If it's all blown to smithereens, they might just give up and instead look for the perpetrators. Us."

"Good thinking."

The pair of them headed over to the construction area. Connor took the necessary equipment from his backpack and lay it out on the newly installed plywood floor of the build. With the pair of them, it shouldn't take more than a half hour or so to rig the side of the plat-form nearest the treed perimeter.

When it was completed, they made their way around the perimeter to join with the others.

"Where's Luke?" Connor asked, counting heads.

"The idiot took off a few minutes ago," Ben said, his voice harsh and unyielding.

"What? Where?"

"We don't know," Faraday said. She looked worried, chewing on her bottom lip.

"Damn it. Probably thinks he's going to save his sister," Connor said.

Annoyance filled him even though a part of him totally understood. But the problem was the teenager was jeopardizing their carefully constructed plan, running off half-cocked in a suicidal attempt to be the hero. And now they had two people to rescue.

TWENTY-ONE
CHEYANNE

Day 8: Near Anchor, Alaska
    12:45 a.m.

Cheyanne woke up with a start. She'd been dreaming of better days, time spent with Ty at his place hanging out and fooling around together. Just the two of them like they preferred it. Then she came to consciousness in a new reality. One she already loathed with all her being. All around her, she could hear women sleeping in the dormitory-like atmosphere. Snoring and snuffling in the night like a bunch of animals; she found the sounds annoyed her. Revolting. Why had she done it? Made Ty run away with her? If only she could go back in time, she would never have made her boyfriend leave the sanctuary of the ranch. Then he'd still be alive. Tears slipped out from behind her closed eyes, soaking her pillowcase.

When the storm had passed, she dried her eyes before realizing she needed to use the bathroom. A feeling of dampness between her legs was concerning and she wondered what was going on? No way would she have peed herself. Right?

She sat up and swung her feet over the edge of the bed. Then pulled on her boots. She needed to check what the deal was. She crept through the room toward the doorway, wending her way between the cots.

She stepped carefully out into the hallway and found the guard asleep on a chair, his rifle leaning up against the wall. Was this her big chance? Hardly daring to breathe, she walked on unsteady legs toward the back door, only her fear of discovery keeping her upright. If her dad thought she was trying to escape, she could only imagine his anger at her making him look bad. She learned a few things about him today. Things she found upsetting. The way he was treating the other women bothered her. Sure, they were opportunists, but they were looking to survive too. No way they deserved to be treated so shabbily. He acted like they were there only to do his or his men's biding. Her saving grace was she was his daughter. Otherwise, no knowing what would be happening to her as well. She shuddered thinking of having to service the disgusting pigs at the lodge. They not only smelled bad, but their manners were atrocious, eating like starving buzzards when a plate of food was shoved in front of them.

She made it to the back door, then taking a deep breath while praying no one was on the other side, she eased the doorknob slowly to the right. Knowing it had a tendency to stick from earlier, she pushed her shoulder against it. It squawked loudly in protest in the otherwise quiet night, making the hackles on her neck spring up in horror. She stopped all pretense at being quiet and ran like a bat out of hell for the tree line.

She almost made it. One second she could almost

taste freedom, the next she was grabbed from behind, a movement that spun her around like a rag doll.

"Let me go! I'm bleeding. I need to get help and find out why. I need my grandma. Please, let me go." Cheyanne hated to beg. Every instinct in her made her want to poke his eyes out, kick him in the groin, but he had a tight grip on her jacket. She saw a moment's hesitation in his eyes as she mentioned the blood and she took full advantage. She yanked herself from his grip, half-falling to the ground. But by then, he had pulled up his rifle and had it pointed in her direction.

"Okay," he grunted. "I'll take you to the outhouse, but that's as far as you go, little girl."

She shivered in her parka, feeling the bitter wind that had begun to blow since she'd gone to bed. She was forced to lead the way around the lodge and over to the offensive outhouse, wishing there was some way to get away from the asshole. She slipped inside the stinky space, startled by a hand slipping over her mouth as the door shut behind her. She was about to scream when she heard a familiar voice whisper in her ear.

"It's me, Luke. Promise not to raise the alarm if I let go of your mouth?"

She nodded. He cautiously pulled his hand away and she half-collapsed in his arms, hugging him tightly. "You came. I need to get out of here. I made a stupid mistake. Ty's dead because of me." The tears flowed again and her brother looked stricken by her confession.

"What happened?"

"Some gang of men on the road shot at us. They wanted the horses and our stuff. I barely made it away." Bile rose in the back of her throat as she was forced to relive the desperate situation for the umpteenth time. If only she had shot them all, Ty would be safe. She imagined having an automatic rifle that would mow them all down in seconds. It helped, the visualization easing the pain of Ty's death.

"You're lucky to be alive. A lot of bad people out there now. Braveheart's the only safe place I know of."

"I get that. I wanna go back with you."

"We all came to help you. Connor and Sam. Some new people, Jake, Ben, and Faraday came to help as well. We want you to come home with us. Everyone's so worried about you. We have a good plan. We're going to get you away from here."

Cheyanne only recognized two names on her brother's list, but she let it go. He said they were new. Introductions could wait until later though she was curious about them. The very fact they had come to help her was what mattered, even the great Connor Hale who she had hated with all her heart up till now was here. She didn't know what to make of it. Later. Maybe then she could make sense of it.

"What's the plan?"

"We're creating a diversion and then we're going to wait for you to use the outhouse. Then we rescue you and take you back to the ranch. But I don't know if anyone realizes you're in here right now? They may not be ready to pull it off yet. You might need to come back in a couple of hours."

"I can try. The guard is kind of suspicious." Cheyanne eyed the toilet seat. "I kinda have to go, Luke. Could you turn around or something?"

Her brother did as she asked, shuffling around in the cramped space, and she got down to it. A cramp hit just as she was finishing up, making a moan escape her.

"You okay, sis?"

"Yeah." Though she had no idea if she really was okay.

She was bleeding a little and that couldn't be a good thing. Was the baby all right? She didn't want to jinx anything by saying the words aloud, but she desperately wanted to speak with Laura or her grandma.

"No one's come, so I think you need to go back inside and try again in an hour or two." She hated the idea of having to leave even for a short time and separate herself from her brother. But it was obvious there was no other way.

She nodded. "Fine. I'll do it." She wouldn't even have to fake feeling unwell. An ache was growing in her lower abdomen that made her uneasy.

"Be careful, sis."

"You too, Luke." Cheyanne slipped out the door.

"Took you long enough," the guard complained. He threw a cigarette butt into the snow.

"I'm not feeling very good. My stomach aches. A woman problem." She knew he wouldn't want to discuss it any further. Guys never did.

He stomped along beside her, keeping his distance like she had the plague. Yeah, males were so predictable.

"I'll probably need to go out again later," she said, exaggerating the problem. "I'm bleeding pretty heavily."

He snorted, not saying yes or no. What if he wouldn't let her out again? The thought sent a shard of fear into her heart. No. She had to get out of here. Life was unbearable in this damned place. It felt haunted. Maybe there was something to the rumors of a ghostly spirit that walked the halls of the lodge. The long-dead owner, someone called The Buck, had died here. She dimly remembered the story. It was Connor's mom, Anna Hale, who had taken him down. He'd been a real bad guy back then even though he was the mayor of the town. Killed his wife and her lover. Kidnapped Anna's sister and threw her in the basement. It proved to Cheyanne couldn't trust anyone in authority.

The guard followed her back into the lodge. Then he waited until she was about to enter the room before stepping in front of her and whispering in her ear. "You'd better watch yourself. Your daddy can't always be around keeping your sweet little ass safe."

His words disgusted her, but she needed to be smart and keep a level head. She had to go outside one more time tonight. If she alienated him, she was doomed, much as she wanted to swing an axe and take his leering, fucking head right off. He must have seen some of her anger in her eyes because he backed off and let her slip past him.

She lay back down on her bed, her body aching. She had to count off the minutes now, waiting until she could go outside again. Another cramp hit, harder than the first, and she forced a fist into her mouth to keep from crying out loud.

TWENTY-TWO
LUTHER

Day 8: Hunting Lodge, Near Anchor, Alaska
   1:47 a.m.

Luther was pulled away from a deep sleep, his body screaming at him to empty his bladder. Damn it. He hated what it had come to. Needing to get up in the middle of the night for a piss was beyond humbling. Fucking prostate. And no decent medical help in prison. Fucking guards and doctors didn't care if the men they were in charge of were in pain or not. Rudimentary care was all they offered, and then it was given begrudgingly like they weren't worth treating. In some cases, they had a point. The state was going to take their lives anyway, why make it more comfortable or easier for those they were in charge of. But those given life without parole deserved better.

"Why are you awake, baby? Need something?" a groggy female voice asked in the darkness. His thoughts drifted as he tried to ignore the pressure in his groin.

The world was dark again, the way he liked it. A waste of resources, keeping the lights on twenty-four seven at the supermax, just to make lives more miserable. He liked the dark and had missed it inside, for he found it gave him an advantage being hidden from view.

"Gotta take a leak." He threw off the covers and sat up on the edge of the bed. "Go back to sleep."

He stood up and scratched himself. Then he pulled on his pants and boots and threw on his jacket over his bare chest before shambling out into the hall. Luther headed for the back door, not wanting an audience. The front area of the lodge was filled with sleeping bodies.

The moonless night had turned bitter cold making him wish he had a warm sweater under his jacket. He stomped toward the back bushes to take a piss, his ears attuned for any sound. His hearing was one of his superpowers, made up for the state of his prostate at times.

But nothing seemed amiss. Even the animals and birds appeared to have abandoned the location. Hunters were probably the culprit. Only way to feed a family now if you didn't grow your own was to head back into nature and do the dirty work yourself. Not that he was low on provisions, but with his horde of hungry men growing, he might have to secure more supplies sooner rather than later.

He zipped himself up, turning to head back inside when he almost ran into the man who was meant to be guarding Cheyanne's bedroom door. He'd forgotten about it earlier, too groggy from sleep he guessed.

"What are you doing out here?" he growled.

The man looked uneasy, but continued on anyway. "Cheyanne's in the outhouse. She's not feeling well. Cramps or something. Thought you should know, sir."

This wasn't good. Was she losing the baby? If so, this

was really going to upset his daughter. She'd just lost Ty. Damn it. Poor girl. If only her mother hadn't been a skank, she'd be here and able to help her. But no, she'd started up with that asshole and made her children vulnerable with her betrayal. Now she was dead. Fucking bitch.

Luther stomped across the yard toward the outhouse, his anger at the situation making him less cautious. The young guard scurried along after him.

He was about to knock on the door to the biffy when an odd sensation of some subtle shift in the atmosphere made him turn to look toward the opposite end of the compound where the build was happening. He listened carefully, concerned by what could have drawn his attention. Was something or someone out there? Animals had been behaving oddly, birds dropping from the sky. The legendary aurora borealis had not been seen since the incident leaving the land seem emptier some-how, not that he was a superstitious man. Everything had a reason for happening in his opinion. Men like himself had the most reason of all for making things happen to their advantage. Men capable of seeing the big picture.

Ka-boom!

Luther threw himself on the ground as bright flashes of intense light lit the northern night sky. More explosions continued to happen and he hugged the earth as they fired off. Were they under attack? Was this connected to recent events? A cold fear coursed through his body, drenching his skin with icy sweat. Was it all over? A foreign power attacking stateside?

His ears were ringing now, overreacting to the sounds. The young guard had also fallen to the ground and was still lying a few yards to his right. When the cacophony finally stopped and he realized the lodge had not been hit and he was most likely going to live another day, he pushed himself to his feet.

"What the fuck was that?" the guard asked, his eyes wide open, peering all around like any second someone or something was going to leap out at him from the darkness. He held his rifle in his hands, his finger on the trigger.

"Shit! The new build is on fire. We need to alert the others."

"What about Cheyanne?" the guard asked.

"Get her and take her inside, then come back and help. I need all hands on deck to put out that damn fire. And see if you can find some buckets to hold water while you're at it."

"Yes, sir."

Another thought occurred to him as to why this might be happening. "And make sure my daughter stays put inside the lodge. Better tie her to the bed."

"Yes, sir!"

TWENTY-THREE
CHEYANNE

Day 8: Near Anchor, Alaska
   2:57 a.m.

Cheyanne and Luke huddled together inside the outhouse. The explosions had been louder than either of them had expected, making them both shiver with dread. She held on tight to her brother, praying nothing bad was going to happen to the people she cared about.

"Dad will be safe, right?" she asked when the explosions finally ceased. Last thing she wanted to happen was her father being hurt because of her foolish actions. More guilt descended on her shoulders as she realized what her running away had caused for so many people. Stuck in the damn outhouse, the smell overwhelmed her and made her want to vomit again. She clutched at Luke, her belly cramping something awful.

"I think so. Long as he doesn't do something stupid. Or wrong. I mean, this was all meant to be a diversion.

No one will be hurt as long as no one tries to stop us from taking you back home."

"When can we leave?" The walls of the tiny toilet were proving claustrophobic, making her dizzy. She desperately wanted to get the hell out of there. It was all she could manage not to throw open the door and run away.

Suddenly, a loud series of knocks hit the outside of the door, making her cringe. "Get out of there, Cheyanne! We need to get you inside now!"

"Give me a sec!"

"What do we do?" she asked her brother. Her heart rate jacked up and sweat began to pour from her body. She couldn't take this anymore. The world had gone crazy. She had a terrible urge to run and run, to never stop running. She calmed herself down a bit by taking a deep breath, only to be hit by the stench of the place. She gagged, her body spasming.

"I have a gun. If he tries anything, I'll protect you."

Luke's voice was reassuring though they had both been speaking softly to avoid detection. But it was so tight in the outhouse. Would he be able to react quick enough to stop the guard from shooting them once the guard realized she and Luke were in there together?

"What do you want me to do?" she asked. "Do you have a weapon for me?"

"Here, take this." He handed her an eight-inch knife he pulled from the sheath strapped around his waist. "Squeeze yourself into the corner. I'll go out first."

She could hear loud shouting, angry men trying to deal with things. Luther's crew must be running around now. Good. Give those lowlifes something else to focus on. She moved as tight to the sidewall as possible, but it barely made a difference. She could be easily be hit with a bullet if the guard opened fire. She had to pray he wasn't that stupid or desperate.

"Okay. I'm going to open the door. Are you ready?" Luke said.

"I love you, Luke!"

He gave her a tight smile in return. "Love you too, sis."

Cheyanne held her breath as her brother sprang into action. He kicked the door wide open, knocking into the guard standing on the other side. The man's gun fired off, a bright flash that went upward in the darkness, missing them both. Luke stepped out. She stayed inside the small space, transfixed by the sight of the burning lumber in the distance. The shapes of downed trees littered the outer perimeter of the compound. Men were running toward the fire, some carrying buckets, others weapons. Most of the ex-cons were looking away from her and Luke.

Her eyes shot back to her brother and the guard. They were now locked in mortal combat.

"Run, Cheyanne!" Luke screamed. His hands were busy trying to take down the asshole. The grunts of the two men fighting for their lives filled her ears. She wanted to run in the worst way, but she couldn't leave her brother. No way. Look what happened when she ran away from Ty. He'd been killed, something she might never be able to forgive herself for. *I have to do something. Anything. But what?*

Lurching from the safety of the small building, she moved around the pair, desperate for a chance to use the knife. Last thing she wanted to do was hit her brother by accident. Spying the guard's rifle lying half-buried in the snow, she edged around the grabbing pair and picked it up. Better than a knife. She brought it up to focus the barrel on the guard who was preventing them from leaving, her throat tightened by fear. Could she do it? Shoot the man in cold blood?

The guard appeared to be getting the upper hand, his hands around her brother's neck. He was larger and stronger than Luke who was a teenage boy, likely also experienced at hand-to-hand combat from being in person. She had to do something. Now. She pulled the trigger.

The sounds of the bullets were deafening. When she opened her eyes, the two men had fallen to the ground. Had her shots gone astray? Was Luke hurt?

She fell to her knees and crawled over to the pair. Luke was lying underneath the guard, trying to push his heavy body off him. She lent her strength to assisting him, and between them they managed to roll the man off him.

"Are you okay?"

"Yeah, I think so, but he's not," he said with a hoarseness to his voice. "Good shooting, sis."

Luke rubbed at his neck, then got to his feet. "We gotta get out of here."

They raced toward the trees farthest away from the fire, both holding their weapons tight in their hands. As they ran away, she prayed no one would see them and try to stop them from leaving. Adrenaline was riding so high in her she felt invincible for the first time in her life. Let them try. She had a gun, same as them. She'd just shot a man. She'd proved she could handle herself.

Then realization hit. She'd actually killed someone. Taken their life. A person who would never see a sunrise ever again. Be with family. Experience love. No. All that had been stripped away in a few seconds. A sick feeling turned her stomach and before she could reach the safety of the trees, her body rejected the idea of what she had done to survive. Suddenly she was spewing the food she'd had for supper, splashing the contents all over the snow.

Luke grabbed her arm. "Sorry, sis. We got to keep moving before someone spots us."

She nodded and made her feet move a few more steps. If they could only reach the safety of the trees. Her breath ragged, the pair of them finally slipped inside the forest's edge. She glanced back at the harrowing scene of desolation, visible through the tree trunks. The fire still burned brightly, making the faces of those trying to put it out look somehow unholy. Like a scene from Dante's Inferno, a poem she'd studied in school. Horrifying and strangely beautiful all at the same time.

"What the fuck are you two doing over here?" a loud voice demanded from nearby. Cheyanne spun around only to be confronted by another man with an assault rifle pointed directly at them.

She cursed the bad luck even as another more powerful cramp powered its way through her belly. It was all she could do to stay on her feet.

"You going somewhere, Cheyanne? I don't think Daddy would like that."

It was one of the men from the lodge. The asshole was always leering at her or the other women. Creepy asshole.

"I go where I want," she shot back. "Move away or we'll shoot."

"Yeah, right. You're just a pair of kids," he scoffed. "You haven't got the guts to shoot a full-grown man."

Crack. Crack.

A blast of gunfire pierced the night and the piece of shit juddered to the ground. *I may be a kid, but I know how to shoot bad guys.* The satisfaction was short-lived. Luke gave her a look of surprise, then slumped to the ground.

"Luke, are you all right?" She was instantly at his side, checking to see if he had been hit. Had the man managed to get a shot off as well?

"I can't see! My eyes…" Luke raised a hand to his face. Blood was flowing from a wound on the side of his head. Filled with horror, she froze. Her stomach clenched down hard on itself, but she had nothing left to throw up. She swallowed against the bile. *What should I do?* She needed to act. Now. Her mind cleared as the answer came to her.

"We have to keep pressure on it. You're bleeding. What can I use?"

"My scarf."

She tugged the wool scarf from around his neck and pressed it to the open wound on the side of his head. Luke winced. "Why can't I see? Is there blood in my eyes? Get me some water. Maybe rinsing them will help."

"Where's the water, Luke?"

"In my pack."

He rolled over enough she could reach the water bottle. He grabbed it and sat up abruptly, flooding his eyes with the water, then blinking rapidly.

"I still can't see. What's wrong with me?"

"We need to get help. I'll lead you out of here. Let me tie the scarf around your head."

Her heart was thumping so hard against the walls of her chest it felt about to burst. She went about the business of tying the scarf carefully around her brother's head. She wanted to shoot the motherfucker all over again for what he had done to Luke. *Please let him be okay.* Guilt curdled her stomach and if she had anything left in her, she'd be throwing up all over again.

"You'll have to carry the rifles, sis." Her practical brother spoke up, giving her something to keep her mind occupied.

Cheyanne picked up his weapon and slung it over her back. She gave her brother a hand up, then picked up her own long gun, keeping it at the ready.

"We gotta get out of here," she said. "Where do we go?"

"Head south. The Shark is in that direction. There's a first aid kit there."

Luke reached out a hand and she directed him to hold on to her coat.

Cheyanne dug deep inside herself and used what little energy she had to keep one foot moving in front of the other. Her brother was pressed close to her side, stumbling along in the darkness. She was the cause of all this. If she hadn't run away, none of this would have happened. *God, if you're listening, please help Luke.* She had gotten her brother shot. Could it get any worse?

TWENTY-FOUR
CONNOR

Day 8: Near Anchor, Alaska
   3:07 a.m.

The sounds of gunfire echoed in the distance, emitting flashes of light near the lodge. Were Luke and Cheyanne in trouble? The foolish yet brave young man had taken it upon himself to rescue his sister. Stupid kid. A part of Connor understood, admired the action even, while another condemned it. Now he had two teenagers to worry about. And both had been given over to his charge. Dan and Jean would never forgive him if anything happened to either of them.

Their plan was working. Most of the ex-cons were busy dealing with the fire. They'd set up a relay of sorts, hauling buckets and containers of water to pour over the burning lumber. He'd been right about a smaller explosion being better to keep the men occupied. Otherwise, they'd just give up in panic and be seeking revenge against the perpetrators.

Connor was headed for the outhouse, but now he increased his speed. He raced through the trees, careful as possible with the placement of his footsteps in an effort to avoid a fall. In the darkness a pair of shadowy figures emerged from behind a tree, backlit by the fire making it difficult to make out who it was. One appeared to be holding on to the other one, one held a rifle pointed his way. It took a second for him to realize one of them was female.

"Luke, Cheyanne?" he asked.

"Don't shoot! Luke's hurt," Cheyanne called out.

"Damn it." Connor raced to the teenagers' side, grabbing hold of Luke's arm with his free hand. "What happened?"

"A guard shot him. He can't see anything."

Connor peered into the forest, seeking out any movement or threat. "Did the man follow you?"

"No. He's dead."

Cheyanne's voice was flat, like she was suppressing her emotions. Had she killed a man tonight? A small moan escaped her, and she pressed a hand to her belly making him forget about the guard for the moment.

"Are you okay?" Had she been shot as well?

"I don't know. It started before all this happened."

"We got to get you out of here. Can you walk?"

"Yeah, I can manage." The teen's face was dead white in the darkness, her eyes dark pools. She didn't have her usual snarky attitude and while it was welcomed, he could only imagine what she had gone through to not be all up in his face, but actually trying to cooperate. Hell of a way to achieve it.

The scarf tied over Luke's eyes had him worried. How bad was it?

"Let's get moving. I'll lead, Luke." The teenager was quiet, but he nodded his head in agreement.

The three of them began the trek back to join the others. They planned to meet up at The Shark, once Cheyanne was rescued. Sam and Mike, Ben and Faraday, were on the south side of the compound, prepared to begin shooting if Connor came under attack rescuing the teenagers. They were going to act as a decoy, leading the gunfire away from the outhouse and further to the west. Luke's decision had been the only wrench in the plan, but he had to admit it had worked. He'd been able to talk his sister into leaving. If only he hadn't been shot, all would be unfolding in proper order. Cheyanne's cramps were concerning, but he'd leave that to Laura to deal with. She would be the one, of all of them, the most likely to know what was going on.

"I'm sorry, Luke, it's my fault you got shot."

Cheyanne's voice sounded strangled, like she was having a hard time keeping a lid on her emotions.

"It's not your fault."

"No. It is. If I hadn't run away, none of this would be happening. I shouldn't have done it. It was stupid. Ty's dead because of me too."

The contriteness and heartbreak in her tone took Connor by complete surprise even as he absorbed the intel on her boyfriend. It sounded like she'd grown up some in the past couple of days. He felt for her. Getting her brother shot would haunt her the rest of her life. He could only hope the sight issue wasn't permanent and that something could be done.

"You didn't kill Ty or cause Luke to be shot. Others made the decision." He offered what little he had. Unfortunately, it was partly true. But she was a teenager, prone to making rash decisions. It was a vulnerable and volatile time in life when it was all too easy to fuck up. What teenager hadn't done something they later regretted? The difference was most never paid such a steep price, karma often being kind to the young.

"It's okay, sis. Laura will fix me up."

The bravery in Luke's voice brought a wash of tears to his eyes and he blinked them away. His body went uncomfortably hot, and he took a steadying breath as he guided Luke through the trees. The quicker they all got out of here, the better.

They skirted the compound. A few minutes later, they joined up with the others. His team were occupied watching the actions through the scopes of their rifles, prepared to shoot if necessary.

"It's me, Connor," he said to draw their attention. They could have used those walkie-talkies in the worst way for this mission, but he wouldn't be mentioning them now. Cheyanne had enough guilt to bear.

Sam came forward first, his expression concerned. "Is Luke okay?"

"He was shot. We have to get him back to Braveheart."

"Okay, time to move out," Sam said, alerting the others. Everyone gathered around them, keeping their weapons at the ready.

"Give Cheyanne a hand, she's in pain too," Connor instructed.

"Was she shot?" Sam asked, speaking over her head at him as he stepped over to her side. She was clutching at her belly again, half bent over.

"No. It's something else. We'll talk later," Connor said.

It was a quiet group that made their way through the dark forest. Everyone remained on high alert, expecting some of Luther's men to jump out at them any moment. But the riot they had created was still unfolding in the background, the sounds of panic slowly fading as they hurried toward the safety of the waiting vehicle.

Not far now. Another hundred yards and they'd be in the clear.

Realizing they were so close to getting away increased everyone's speed. Then Luke stumbled and half dropped to his knees. Connor had to keep his impatience at bay as he helped the youngster regain his footing, wanting to pick him up and carry him the remaining distance. Cheyanne was in even worse straits. Moaning and half bent over.

"Fuck this," Sam said.

He handed his rifle off to Jake. He picked up the young girl and began to cart her through the snow. She protested weakly, but held on to him. His actions allowed them to move quicker. Connor was considering doing the same when gunshots alerted them to company.

"Hurry!" he shouted, giving up all pretense of hiding their actions. Once they reached the safety of The Shark, they would be home free.

Fifty yards.

The team raced even quicker at his command. Everyone knew it was life or death. The ex-cons at the compound were the most ruthless of all men, the dregs of society. They would sooner kill his people than anything. Maybe they would try to keep the teenagers alive, but having to live in squalor was a bad fate for them as well, at the mercy of bad men.

With each step the sense of being observed and under attack increased. Who was shooting at them? He couldn't see anyone yet, though his neck was a swivel.

A series of automatic fire made his pulse ratchet up. Damn it. They were flanking them.

Thirty yards.

"I'm going to draw them off," Jake said, breaking away from the group.

"No! Keep running!" Connor shouted. Last thing he wanted was to leave a man behind.

But Jake made good on his word. He went down on one knee and began shooting at the flashes of gunfire. Ben veered off to the opposite side and did the same.

Ten yards.

The last few feet felt an eternity. Connor yanked open the passenger door and unceremoniously helped Luke inside. "Get in!"

He quickly assisted Sam with Cheyanne, then turned back to check on Jake and Sam. Both were moving backward through the snow, still shooting at the unseen intruders. Faraday was also part of the equation now, holding the middle section, careful not to shoot at either of the flanking men.

The ex-cons were visible as they made their way into the clearing. At least six of them, all holding weapons and firing in their direction. They were bunched up, meaning they had no military training.

"Hurry up!"

Faraday glanced back at him, realizing everyone was safe. She turned and raced toward the vehicle, jumping inside to join them.

Jake and Ben worked like an efficient team; their tactical training evident in their every action. They picked off a couple of the men, their bodies dropping into the snow. The others pressed forward.

Ben reached them first. He continued firing as Jake

caught up. With one last burst of gunfire, the pair jumped inside The Shark, slamming the door shut.

Fuck. They had made it. Barely believing no one else got shot, Connor took a deep breath.

He started the engine and thrust it in gear, directing the heavy armored vehicle away from the woods and onto the back road they'd entered by. Now they had to worry about how badly off the pair of teenagers was.

"How are they?" he asked, careful to keep his full attention on the road.

Ben spoke up, the one team member with good medical training. "They'll make it. Just keep driving." Though his words were positive, he could hear traces of concern underlying them. They needed to get the siblings home and have a good look at them ASAP.

Connor turned his mind back to his driving, all he could do was to get them home in one piece. There could be pursuit. Did the men recognize his team? If so, they could very well lead them back to Braveheart. The new worry grabbed him by the throat. Fuck. Life was never going to be the same. Then he calmed himself. He had to be a leader, meaning he had to stay in control at all times, no matter the cost. At that moment he felt the presence of his dad nearby. The man who had shown him how to be a man. Not by talking, but in his actions. Do or die. There was nothing else for it.

TWENTY-FIVE
LUTHER

Day 8: Hunting Lodge, Near Anchor, Alaska
   3:47 a.m.

"What the fuck happened?" Luther was incensed. The top of his head felt like it might blow off at any second. "Where is my daughter?"

"We have a team out looking for her, sir."

Gunfire echoed in the distance. Both men turned toward the sound. The compound was in chaos. The burning structure only half out, with flames licking at the two-by-fours. Fuck! They'd lost a lot in the attack. It would set them back for days. Most of what had already been built would be a write-off. Efforts and valuable resources. Lost forever. Who had done this? He would see them pay, and pay dearly.

"Where's the guard who was meant to be guarding my daughter? Find him." If he couldn't get his hands on the men responsible for this mayhem, then he would enjoy killing the man who hadn't done his duty and protected Cheyanne.

"Yes, sir."

The soldier took off and began searching around the area of the outhouse, looking for footprints. Luther waited impatiently for the man to return, his mind racing with thoughts of what to do next. Diego was a few days out according to his last message. But now he wouldn't have the necessary quarters for housing the man and his soldiers. This was bad. Worse, it made him look bad, not fit to be trusted to provide what was most needed. A proper, functioning hideout with the basics of survival close at hand. Housing. Food. Guns. Now some asshole had taken away the housing his men had worked so hard to finish before the cartel bosses' arrival. The seriousness of the situation was not lost on him. If he couldn't provide it here, then he would have to provide it elsewhere. But how? Cheyanne had been his ticket into Braveheart. She would have been the perfect decoy to allow him access. Now she was gone. And a couple of his scouts had come back from the ranch with bad news. The wall was unscalable, not only razor wired, but electrified.

Luther's mood soured further when the man came back at a jog only to announce he'd found a body.

"Someone shot him. Then took off into the woods."

"God damn it!" He was incensed. He had to do everything himself. "Let's go. We're going to find them and get to the bottom of this. Find out where they're headed. Go get me a proper flashlight."

The soldier did his biding, took off at a run and then raced back, handing him what he needed.

It was easy enough to follow the trail. Two figures, steps so close it was obvious one was helping the other.

Had the guard managed to shoot one of them? Good. It would slow them down. They weren't a hundred yards from the lodge when a small group of his men appeared through the trees, easily recognizable by their orange neon hats he'd made them wear.

Luther stalked toward them, his anger making him focus on only one thing. Revenge. "Tell me what happened? Who's responsible?"

"I recognized that man you showed us a photo of in jail. The guy you said was responsible for your being in prison. I've forgotten his name, sir."

"Fucking Connor Hale." He should have guessed. To think the asshole came and stole his daughter right out from under his eyes. On his watch too. An anger like he'd never known came over Luther. One so powerful he couldn't see anything around himself except a red haze. If he ever got his hands on the man, he would rip him a new one. But first he would skin him alive, then...

"Are you all right, sir?"

"Yeah. Anything else?" He forced himself to calm down, to listen. He needed intel.

"I think your son was with them. He was the one with your daughter."

"Luke. How many others?"

"We counted six. Five guys and one female. All heavily armed. We lost two of our own. Owen and Greg. Bastards shot them. But one of theirs was wounded. Looked like he was shot in the head."

"How did they get away?" Last he knew, Connor only had horses. That was how his daughter and Ty had arrived.

"They were driving this huge monster of a vehicle. All armor plated. Fucking something, boss. No bullets could penetrate its skin."

He didn't appreciate the praise for his enemy's acquisition. In fact, it downright irked him.

"What do you want us to do, sir?"

What to do? There wasn't enough time to rebuild, so that meant acquiring a new place. An idea popped into his head, fully realized making him once more think he must be a fucking genius among men to be able to see the big picture so clearly. Quickly. A bit of intel from the past and how to access a fortress gave the answer he needed. Every place had its weak point. Somewhere either unguarded or more readily assessable to the enemy. Braveheart, strong as all the precautions had been, wasn't invincible. No place was. So, if he couldn't go over, and couldn't use Cheyanne as a bargaining chip, that left only one thing to do to gain entry.

"Gather up all the men. I have a new plan. The perfect solution. We'll work in relays and get this job done before reinforcements arrive."

The team looked mystified, but he didn't bother to explain. He'd share it with all of them at the same time.

Luther led the march back into the compound. They had just over forty-eight hours to complete the job. Did he have enough bodies? It would be close, but not impossible if everyone did their part. If not, then they would bear the full extent of his wrath. Do or die.

TWENTY-SIX
CHEYANNE

Day 8: Braveheart Horse Ranch
   4:46 a.m.

"What happened?" Grandpa Dan came out onto the porch to greet them, his expression filled with anxiety. Cheyanne had no words for him. She tried to follow the others inside, but he grabbed her arm.

"What happened to Luke?" he asked, holding tightly to her sleeve. A blaze of anger rose inside her. All he cared about was Luke. Not her. Nothing had changed. Grandma Jean came rushing into the living room from the kitchen. She glanced at Connor, Sam, and Ben escorting her brother into the living room, then over at Cheyanne.

"He got shot, okay? He was trying to help me and some asshole shot him." She pulled away from her grandpa's grip and hurried after the others. Grandma Jean stepped into her path.

"Thank God you're home safe and sound," she said,

enveloping her in a tight bear hug. She got caught off guard, breathing in her grandma's comforting flowery scent always accompanied with a touch of lemon from her favorite dish soap. Tears filled her eyes and she blinked them away. She didn't deserve this. Not after what she had done.

"I'm sorry." She pulled away and hurried after her brother.

"What's wrong with Luke?" Grandpa asked. He entered the kitchen on her heels, a scowl on his wrinkled face.

Cheyanne could only stand and watch as Ben went to work on her brother. Her mind was too occupied, too worried about Luke to register the pain that still tugged at her abdomen, though it felt less than before.

Ben ordered a bowl of warm water, clean cloths, and their medical kit to be brought to the table. Unwrapping the scarf she had tied around her brother's head, she let out a small gasp at the deep wound that furrowed the side of his skull. His hair was matted with blood and his shirt had soaked up more of it. The bullet's path was just above his ear, taking out part of his temple. One eye was filled with blood. Tears of blood ran down his face, his expression half-panicked.

"I can't see anything!" He clawed at his face and Connor quickly intervened, pulling his hands away.

"Don't touch the wound, Luke. Ben will take care of you. He knows his business." His tone was firm but caring. The man she had spent months detesting above all others had come to her rescue. But why did he have to put her brother in such mortal danger? A sudden surge of anger rose up, though a part of her knew she was being unfair. Her brother had come along because he would have insisted. Yeah, but Connor's the adult, she reasoned. He should have stopped him.

Then she forgot all that and went down on both knees to grab Luke's hands. "It's going to be okay, bro. Let them fix you up. You'll be able to see soon."

"Promise?"

"I pinky swear promise." Her throat tightened with more tears as she had to help him find her pinky finger because he was in the dark. She couldn't even begin to imagine what he was going through. To not be able to see. That was her worst nightmare. In the new reality they had been forced into, seeing was even more essential than before. How else to protect yourself if you couldn't see the enemy coming?

"He'll need something for the pain," Ben announced.

Connor rolled up her brother's sleeve while Ben pulled out a syringe and poked it into the head of a vial. He drew out a few CCs of clear liquid before injecting it into Luke's inner arm. Then he set to work cleaning and stitching the ugly wound. Even after her brother's eyes were flushed out again with saline, he looked terrified and she knew he couldn't see anything. She held on to his hands during the entire procedure, trying to offer what comfort she could. Finally, it was done and Ben wove clean bandages around his head and over his eyes. Heartsick, she got up from her knees and fell into a kitchen chair.

This was all her fault.

If only she had stayed at the ranch, none of this would have happened. What if Luke was permanently blind? What then? She was responsible for his getting shot and knew she loved her brother above everyone else, even her father, much as he drove her crazy at times with his rose-colored view of the world. She vowed right then and there to never leave his side. She would be his eyes, from now on. At least until he could see again. She pulled on the heavy mantle of responsibility willingly, knowing she had to make it up to him. Give up her own life if necessary to make sure Luke was okay.

A hand dropped onto her shoulder. Cheyanne looked up to see her grandma looking down at her with compassion. She swallowed. Afraid to talk and give away her fear and doubts. "Don't be blaming yourself, sweetheart. You couldn't know. Plus, you have a baby to think about. Stress is not good for you or it. I believe it leads to colicky little ones. You don't want that."

Cheyanne startled. "You knew?"

"Yes. You've been eating like a horse. Packing it away like there's no tomorrow. And you have a glow about you."

Now that the secret was exposed, she felt some of her burden lift. Even the crushing cramps had receded. Maybe she should mention the problem to her grandma in private? But compared to Luke's injuries, it seemed unimportant now. All she wanted to do was sleep for days. The adrenaline rush of earlier receded so quickly the room began to spin like she was drunk.

"How are you doing, Cheyanne? You were in terrible pain earlier?" Connor's sharp eyes bore into hers. She shook her head, not wanting to talk about it. She swayed in her seat. Then everything went dark.

TWENTY-SEVEN
MCKENNA

Day 8: Braveheart Horse Ranch
   5:44 a.m.

The sounds of the front door opening woke Mckenna from the shadow-filled sleep she'd fallen into. She sat up, letting the blanket drop away, still dressed in her clothes. She was resting on the sofa in the living room, unwilling to go to bed until she'd seen with her own two eyes that Connor was back safe and sound. She pushed her feet into her shoes and got up, using the crutches for support.

Hurrying into the kitchen, she found Connor opening a cupboard door and pulling out a bottle of scotch. He caught her movement and set the bottle down, striding over to take her into his arms.

She nestled in tight against him, listening to the reassuring thump of his heartbeat. It sounded so strong, like it could go on forever. "Thank goodness you're okay," she whispered.

He pulled back enough to kiss her. When they finally

broke apart, she looked him in the eye and saw the devastation clear as day. "Are you okay?"

He shook his head and went back to the counter, ready to pour a glass of the amber liquid. "Want one?"

"Yeah, I think I do."

She waited until he had a couple of swallows of the potent liquor before asking, "What went down?"

"Luke got hurt. Side of his head, says he can't see anything."

The stark words hollowed her out. "Poor kid. What does Ben say?"

"Too soon to say. Everyone's upset about it. And rightly so, it should never have happened. If only I'd kept a tighter rein on him and never let him out of my sight. Damn foolish kid wanted so badly to save his sister he took chances. If only he'd waited, none of this would have happened."

"What did he do?"

He explained, his expression so bleak she felt his pain. "He did help though. Warned Cheyanne and helped save the day. Don't take the sacrifice away from him."

"But I can't have him running off and doing something like that again."

She laid a hand over his. She knew how important it was for Connor that everyone stay safe on his watch, but sometimes it wasn't possible. The reality of this new world they had been thrust into meant sometimes people would have to take chances. Deem it necessary on their own. Like she had done back in the woods on their way to Ben's place when he'd gotten so upset about her coming back for him. It had caused their first and only argument to date. "Let him have this. Yes, he should have followed your orders. But he didn't. Nothing's going to change that. If you bring him to task on it, he'll only feel worse. He needs our support now. Others will learn more from what happened to him than by anything you could say."

He looked at her now, really looked at her. "You're a wise woman, Mckenna. The years have been good to you."

"I don't know about that." She was uncomfortable under his scrutiny and took another swallow of the scotch. "But I did have a good teacher in Grandma McTavish. She called it like she saw it."

Wulver began barking loudly outside, drawing both of their attention. Connor's demeanor immediately changed. He stood up and moved efficiently over to the door, donning his outerwear in seconds before picking up his Bergara-Highlander he kept on a rack beside the entrance along with other assorted weaponry. She didn't find it strange. Her ex had kept guns all over the house, always prepared for an attack in Mexico.

"Wait here."

She didn't say anything, but knew she would also be arming herself the second he slipped outside. This was a different time. Yes, he would do his best to keep everyone safe. But so would those in his sphere do all they could to have his back. He'd just have to get used to it. As terrible as Luke's shooting was, she understood his actions. Everyone was all in now.

She got up and went to the kitchen window, drawing the curtain aside. She'd keep an eye on the situation and only intervene if it was necessary. Two male figures joined Connor in the yard, making her relieved others already had his back. They disappeared from view and she had to make up her mind then if she should head out or not.

A faint cry from the second floor settled the situation. She hurried up the staircase to check on Lily. Then she remembered she could see the front yard from his bedroom. Mckenna made an about-face and went back and grabbed another weapon from his stockpile to add to her firepower.

Lily was also used to weaponry spread around the house. Her holding a sleek black sub-machine in her hands wasn't so far out of the ordinary. She set it down near the doorway and hurried to her daughter's side.

She was sitting up, clutching her teddy bear, her eyes wide open. "I dreamed Daddy was here. I was scared."

Her daughter's small high-pitched voice cleaved her heart in two. "Oh sweetheart, no, he's not here. But Mommy is." She sat down on the edge of the bed and smoothed Lily's tangled curls. She had said she was scared. Did she mean she was frightened of her father? Had she remembered something from Mexico? Her ex was a bad man, growing worse over her daughter's early years of childhood.

She tucked Lily back under the covers along with her bear, then kissed her forehead. "Go to sleep now, princess. I'll stay with you."

What was going on outside? She desperately wanted to look out the window, but Lily needed her. It seemed like an eternity but was only a few minutes later when her daughter slipped back to sleep.

She eased herself out of bed and crept to the window. Pulling the drape aside, she picked up the binoculars lying on the windowsill and stared out into the yard.

It was quiet now, no sign of anyone or anything moving about though she could see halfway down the road leading to the wall. Connor had been smart to build a wall separating himself from the outside world. He had prepared for this disaster, far more than most. She could only imagine people down to their last package of KD or tin of something unknown from the back of the pantry. It had been eight days and well past the time of everyone having used up what they had on hand, at least according to all the statistics she had read.

Sounds emanated from the downstairs, drawing her attention. Her pulse increased. Was it friend or foe? She crept from the room, picking up the assault rifle on her way out the bedroom door and down the staircase. From the sounds of the voices, they were in the kitchen, but they sounded friendly enough. She took a deep breath and came around the corner to peer into the room.

Connor was interacting with what looked like a family. A middle-aged couple and a pair of very droopy looking teenagers.

"Mckenna." Connor caught sight of her hovering nearby. "We've got some new people joining us. I'd like you to meet them. This is the sheriff I told you about. Sheriff Brady, his wife Marilyn, son Jamie and daughter Layla. They'll be staying with us in the house."

"Nice to meet you." She laid the gun aside and stepped forward to shake the man's hand, keeping her balance with the crutches. She liked the look of him. Solid. Dependable. He appeared to have his act together. His wife held back as did the two teenagers who only spared a mutinous glance her way for a second before ignoring all the adults. Yeah, it sucked to be young these days with all the modern conveniences and distractions swept away in a tidal wave they had nothing to do with. It would take time to adapt. But as it was not likely to come back to previous comfort levels in their lifetimes, they might as well make the best of it and not be hard on each other. Lord knows there was enough strife in the world as it was.

"You as well, Mckenna. I hear you had some trouble in Mexico? Then in Golden. I can sympathize. We were in Quinton and it was a terrible disaster after a group of so-called state militia took over and stole everything they could lay their hands on. We barely escaped with our lives. Good people are dead for fighting back." The devastation on the man's face was obvious as he spoke, his eyes hardened by all he had witnessed.

"Connor told me about his time there and what went down. Are you hungry? I could make something to eat. It's almost time for breakfast anyway."

"I need a shower, Mom," the girl whined, ignoring her invite. "I'm filthy. And my feet hurt."

"There's lots of hot water. Let me show you to your rooms. Where do you want them, Connor?" she asked, trying to keep the smile from slipping from her face. Teenagers. No doubt one day Lily would be at that age causing similar havoc. It was then the perilousness of the situation struck home again. There was no guarantee her daughter would get to grow up. She forced her mind away from the terrible thought and kept it focused on the moment. There was nothing else for it. No one knew the future, no matter how some swore they could read it. Right. And she could use two sticks joined together and find water deep underground. Not going to happen. But the image did get her mind away from dwelling on what she could not change.

"There's a guest suite down the hall next to Faraday's that will work well enough with an attached bedroom."

"Do we have to stay here with these people?" the girl asked. "I want to go home. All my friends are in Quinton."

Sheriff Brady looked like he'd had enough, his face darkening. She could only imagine what these past few days had been like with the high-needs teenager. She upped her game then, wanting to bring some peace to the situation for the poor man. He'd done his duty, just getting them to the ranch.

"Come with me, Layla. We've got some nice grooming products you might be interested in. Bath salts. Skin lotions. The good brands. Connor really stocked up on some things you might enjoy."

"I need my makeup. Dad made me leave without it." It would be a funny situation, if only it wasn't so tragic. The poor girl couldn't see past the ring attached to the end of her nose. Lily had herself together better most of the time. She hoped it stayed that way for her little girl.

"Makeup might be a bit hard to come by, but you're so young and pretty, you hardly need anything." She made certain to add a certain brightness to her tone and escorted the young girl, followed closely by her mother.

"I'll be back in a sec to start breakfast," she said, though a wave of weariness came over her. She was running on empty. Well, so was everyone else. This was the time that showed the metal you were made of. Either you could dig down deep and find the strength and will to keep control of yourself. Or not.

TWENTY-EIGHT
CONNOR

Day 8: Braveheart Horse Ranch
6:27 a.m.

"We gotta talk," Brady said, pulling him aside as the rest of his family followed Mckenna from the room.

"Wanna drink first?" Connor asked. Brady had already filled him in on how he and his family had hitched a ride on an old hay wagon pulled by draft horses and driven by a farmer. The man had been on his way to Anchor to rescue his daughter and had picked them up not far outside of Quinton on their first day on the road. In reality, they'd only had to walk the thirty miles to the ranch. They had been lucky, catching a ride, but he didn't think Brady's daughter Layla would agree. Maybe she and Cheyanne would become friends? Or maybe he should never introduce them. He could only imagine the fireworks or trouble that pair could instigate if given full rein.

"Yeah." Brady ran a hand over his short hair, his

craggy face seeming to have aged ten years since Connor last saw him in Quinton. "I think we're going to need one while I explain what I found out from the old guy that gave us the lift."

"A lot of shit went down in your old town as well. We passed through there on the way back, tried to stop to see you. We wanted help to get our hands on baby formula and diapers, but were turned away by a bunch of miscreants."

"Baby formula?" Brady took a slug of scotch and made a grimace before setting it back on the table. "Good liquor, I needed that."

"Yeah, I came across a newborn not long after I left Quinton. Eve. She's here now plus another woman I ran into on the journey by the name of Faraday. They're in the room next to yours."

"You tend to attract those in need. Like moths to the flame."

"Good people need to stick together now more than ever. So, let's get right to it. What have you learned?" Much as he was dreading more bad news, there was no avoiding it.

"The 'miscreants' as you called them, they are in complete control of Quinton now, stealing everything not nailed down. But they're there waiting for some larger group to join with, gathering supplies on their behalf. It's an army headed this way. The Martinez Knights is the name I overheard one night on foot patrol, led by some cartel boss named Diego. He has his sights set on joining another crew up in this part of the world. Do you have any idea who that could be?"

The floor figurately dropped away, and Connor felt he was staring into the darkest chasm imaginable. Another cartel group headed this way? Led by Mckenna's ex? Luther was the only logical one he could be meeting. To think those two monsters were going to hook up and try to become the powerhouse up in this part of the world, a world until now had been relatively peaceful. No. It could never be allowed to happen. The very idea was a monstrosity. Vile. A sacrilege on everything in this world that was honorable and right.

Brady was studying him carefully when he snapped out of his immediate stupor at the news. "You know something about this?"

"Yeah. More than I wish I knew. We are directly involved with the very man this Diego is thinking to join with. Luther Meech, a murderer and cartel boss himself, he's staying with his band of ex-cons up north of here. Damn prison set them free when the EMP hit. Living at an old hunting lodge. We burned down a structure he was building there earlier tonight as a decoy. Then rescued his pregnant daughter. Her grandparents and brother live in one of the cottages here."

Brady gave a low whistle, his eyes opening wider, transfixed by the idea for a few seconds. "There is huge trouble on the horizon, buddy."

"If you want to move on, I would understand. A man needs to keep his family safe first and foremost." He had to say it much as he hoped the man would stay. They could use a good man like him at Braveheart, but Brady had to know the danger being at the ranch could cause for him.

"Hell of a game changer. But this place is quite the fortress in its own right. It's a sweet setup you've put together. Good job."

"I also have an underground shelter if worst comes to worst."

"That I would like to see."

"Tomorrow. You should get a few hours rest. Talk this over with your family. I can't ask you to decide now. Sleep on it. We'll talk tomorrow." Connor finished the dregs of his glass.

"Sounds good. I'll admit, these old bones are a bit achy tonight." Brady lumbered to his feet. He rinsed his glass in the sink and set it aside. "Catch you on the other side."

Connor remained behind after the man headed down the hallway to join his family. Mckenna exited the suite a few seconds later. She walked toward him with a smile, bringing a light to his own soul as he watched her navigate efficiently, if not gracefully, with the crutches. In that second, he knew everything he had done and would be asked to do in the future, it was all worth it.

"Get them all settled?" he asked. She leaned down and kissed him fully on the lips, her warm female scent flowing over him. It stirred something deep inside him even as his groin tightened.

"Yes. Now I think we need to do the same." She invited him upstairs with her eyes alone, their smoldering depths promising more. Much more. What a woman. A woman that could have launched a thousand ships. But she wanted to be with him. He was one lucky man. And for this brief moment of time, he would enjoy it. Not think beyond right now. A luxury in a world gone mad.

TWENTY-NINE
LUTHER

Day 8: Braveheart Horse Ranch
    8:01 a.m.

"I've sent a group to Anchor to round up more tools. We'll need pickaxes, shovels, wheelbarrows, lumber and steel plates. Everyone working in teams round the clock. What I wouldn't do for a working excavator. Or a crane," Tom said. The guy had turned into a decent replacement for Thomas number one. Kept his nose clean and stayed the course.

The pair were surveying the spot chosen earlier for the best likelihood of success for the venture, standing at the farthest reaches of the ranch where the rugged landscape and thick growth of trees obscured the view. Hell, even if they were discovered after they had the steel cover in place, wasn't much Connor could do about it.

"It might take longer to go under, but it's safer than over the top. Conner gets word of this and he'd pick us off one by one. Tell the men we gotta keep the noise down to a bare minimum. No talking or fooling around. Tell them it's like you're digging your way out of prison and all the guards are listening, except we're actually going to be taking over the joint," Luther said. "And kill the guards."

"That'll work. We'll be like ninjas. Coming in the night when there's fuck all anyone can do anything about it," Tom said with a cold grin.

Luther mounted his horse, more than satisfied with the plan. He enjoyed riding one of Connor's former horses. One more thing he'd managed to take away from the bastard.

"We'll build the cover up at the lodge. Then haul it here in sections. There will be nothing he can do about it. Lessens the risk and keeps it secret longer."

"Will do, boss." Tom pulled himself up into the saddle, looking less than confident at his riding ability, though he was determined to keep his seat. Lot of things men would have to relearn, Luther mused, from horseback riding to how to fabricate from what was available. No longer was anyone going to get the exact parts or material they needed. No, the future belonged to the fabricators and inventors. Those that could create workarounds, unafraid to try it another way.

They headed back in the direction of the lodge, his mind busy considering how best to position himself. Once he had Braveheart, everything would fall into place. Hell, maybe he didn't even need Diego. He had a moment of regret for inviting the man. Things had changed. They didn't need Diego's soldiers as badly as before, war toughened as no doubt they would be. Regional control would be best achieved by one man.

Luther Meech. Diego might not like being his number two. Well, if he caused problems, he'd go the way of Connor Hale.

THIRTY
CHEYANNE

Day 8: Braveheart Horse Ranch
   11:11 a.m.

Cheyanne woke up discombobulated, her heart skittering. A clammy sweat had broken out all over her body. She shivered violently trying to escape the terrifying images. Shadows had been chasing her in the dark, dissolving before again reappearing and warping into ghost-like figures. They scared her to the core. Red eyes stared at her through the growing blackness. Devil eyes. But worse yet was the voice, the dead cold voice of a warning like she'd never heard before. *He will come.*

She pushed her disheveled hair back from her sweaty face and took a deep breath. It felt like a terrible premonition, like right out of a fantasy 3D storybook. Worse. It had actually happened, right? She took a few breaths to calm herself. It was only a nightmare, nothing more. Then she remembered the events of the night before. *Luke.*

She clamored off the bed and scrambled down the hallway to her brother's room. The door was closed. She hesitated at opening it and going inside. What if he were sleeping? He needed his rest to recover. Ben had explained how important it was.

"Cheyanne." Grandma Jean shuffled up to her, her expression pensive but calm, her tone quiet and reassuring. "Come. Let your brother rest. And you need to eat something."

"I'm not hungry." She stood there in the hallway, uncertain of what to do next. She felt two forces were at work inside her. Always had been. A war had been going on for longer than she could remember. One part of her still wanted to run away as fast as she could, no denying it, the other, stronger than before, speaking up a little louder now, wanted her to try harder to do the right things to help her family. No denying she had not always been there for them, much as she loved them all.

"You need to think of the baby."

Her grandma was right. She bit her lip, wishing she could have a do-over. But life was not a dress rehearsal. There were no do-overs. Tears slipped from behind her closed eyes and she felt herself shaking. What had she done?

"Come, child. Leave your brother to sleep. Some warm milk and a sandwich will help you feel better. I just took some fresh loaves out of the oven. There are some cinnamon buns for dessert. First come, first served."

Cheyanne gave her grandma a shaky smile even as the scent of yeasty bread filled her with a warmth that brought a rush of tears to her eyes. She was grateful to be home, not that she deserved it. "I'm sorry, Grandma."

They moved down the hallway toward the kitchen,

leaving Luke to rest. She realized she was taller than her grandma now. The older woman who had been such a main force in her life had always seemed larger before today, now it was as if she had shrunk a bit in stature, her back bowed. A sense of time slipping through her fingers brought another round of worry. She shuffled along at her grandma's pace, wishing for things that could never be.

"I know, child. The lessons of life are so often earned in blood and pain. There's nothing for it but to move forward. Luke will need us to be strong for him now. The women in our family we know how to be strong. We come from hardy pioneer stock, many generations ago, back to the early days of settling this country. You've got strong mettle inside you. It's in your blood. It's what's made it hard for you to accept things. But it's also what will allow you to pick up the pieces and make the best of life."

"I never wanted to hurt my family. But I wanted a place of my own. A place for Ty, me and the baby."

"Plenty of time for your own place later on. Right now, the world the shape it's in, you need to be with your own people. Grandpa and I won't be around forever."

"Don't say that. I need you."

"Not going to happen tomorrow, child. I got a few good years left in me. And I'm looking forward to my first great-grandbaby. I can't leave this world until I see it safely here."

Yes. She had to start focusing on the baby. Ty was dead. No changing that. Luke was hurt, but maybe he would recover okay. Ben said it was possible. The blindness might not be permanent. She was home again. Surrounded by people she loved and could count on. She needed to focus on becoming a better person now. Help out her grandma more. But that darn lazy Brandi better do more or she would see to it that she got hers. Just because she was going to try harder with her own flesh and blood, didn't mean she had to try with outsiders. Even Connor didn't want his own brother and sister-in-law in his house. Her grandma had mentioned last night they'd been moved into a house similar to the one her family occupied. Good. Now they were equals. Hell, better than equals. Cheyenne could work circles around the woman if she put her mind to it. She had a few months before the baby was born. She'd start pulling her end of the load beginning today.

She swept into the kitchen and turned to her grandma. "Sit down, Grandma. My turn to serve you. I'm going to make us tea and sandwiches. I'm feeling much better now."

Her grandma rewarded her with a tired smile, making her faded blue eyes sparkle for a moment. She did as Cheyenne requested, even easing off the slip-on shoes from her swollen feet and wiggling her twisted toes with the painful-looking bunions. She felt her watching as she moved about the spacious country kitchen, filling in the kettle with fresh water and plugging it in. Then pulling out the teapot with the country roses design she knew her grandma cherished and kept for special occasions. In the frig, she found all the fixings for sandwiches and choose a package of ham and cheese, a bag of lettuce, before settling down to work.

"This feels lovely, Cheyenne. I could get used to this."

It was then she realized someone was missing. "Where's Grandpa?"

"He went out earlier to help in the barn. With Luke— well, you know." The reminder of what her brother had been doing to earn his place at Braveheart, his volunteering to work from sunrise to after sunset, hit her hard in the chest, like an actual physical blow. She took a couple of deep breaths, making sure not to let her grandma see how badly it had affected her. She automatically continued her preparation for lunch, incapable of saying anything for the moment.

The door opened and Cheyanne looked over to catch sight of her grandpa Dan entering, his closed expression not boding well. She averted her eyes and continued her task. *Please don't yell at me. I know I did a bad thing.* A few tears dripped onto the counter and she swiped at them angrily. Don't be a big baby. She plated the food, lining up the sandwiches. She'd made extra in case of visitors. Someone always seemed to be hungry and coming in for a free handout from her grandma. It had always been like that. Neighbors dropping in all the time. It was one thing she and Grandma Jean argued about. Now she caught a glimpse of how nice it was to provide something nourishing for others. She would make sure to make the food for Luke from now on. Feed him too until he got better. He had to get better. He just had to.

"Horses are acting spooked today. One caught me in the shin, Jean." It was then she noticed he was limping, favoring his right leg.

Her grandma gave a sigh and slipped her shoes back on. She hurried toward her husband of sixty years and led him to a chair. "Let me take a look."

"Don't be fussing, woman. I'm fine." Cheyanne felt his eyes boring into her back. She set her teeth and turned around, bringing the plate of food over to the table. She hurried back and made the tea, the kettle busy whistling to alert the water was at boiling point.

Her grandpa said nothing, just let his wife roll up his

pant leg to take a good look. "Oh dear, he caught you good. Cheyanne, would you get my first aid kit?"

"Of course." She hurried off to the bathroom to retrieve the small white box with the red cross on top, kept on a shelf in the linen closet. She arrived back in the kitchen just in time to catch a glimpse of the nasty wound. The skin was already dark from the bruising, swollen and very painful looking. A trickle of blood crept down his leg, pooling in his wool sock. Gray with the red toe and heel kind. Her grandma made them for him. Only socks he would wear. He swore all the others were shite.

"What else do you need, Grandma?" she asked.

"Have something to eat. That would please me the most." Grandma Jean spared her a small smile before she went back to tending her husband's leg. "I don't like the look of it. You'll need to keep it elevated, dear."

"I don't have time for that. Not with all that needs doing and fewer hands to do." Though he didn't out and out say it, Cheyanne knew it was her fault.

"I can help, Grandpa," she said, swallowing down her worry and rise of anger at being seen once more as less than in the family. Luke was the golden boy. The one they always counted on to do the right thing while she was this pathetic excuse for a granddaughter who took more than she gave. Well, no more. She was young and strong. She'd show them.

"Okay. You want to help. The barn needs mucking out."

"Now dear—"

"No, she needs to learn what it takes to make a life now. No more coddling, Jean."

THIRTY-ONE
CONNOR

Day 8: Braveheart Horse Ranch
    11:37 a.m.

Wulver at his side, the dog having become much more attached and needy since he'd been away, Connor strode into the barn. He wanted to tend to Loch's flank, check if the wound was healing properly on the proud stallion. With so much coming at him and the others it seemed from every direction since the world had taken a hit it was still reeling from; things were beginning to slide in the barn. He'd noticed it at once. Some of the stalls needed mucking. Tools were in disarray. And the barrels of oats needed refilling from the granary. Nothing a few hours of hard labor couldn't set right.

He'd get at it soon as he checked Loch's condition. Physical labor was a godsend when a man needed time to let his mind rest. Too much had happened of late. He'd been running around acting defensively, not proactively like he preferred. It was advice he'd chosen to live by, the best defense being a good offense. It had given him Braveheart and all its hard-won protections against the onslaught of an unprepared world. He'd built this place from the ground up. Now the fruits of his labor were keeping his people safe, a bastion against a hungry, terrified existence.

After observing Loch was healing fine, he got right down to it. He was just racking the straw and horse droppings from a stall into a wheelbarrow when he caught sight of movement nearby.

He looked up to find Cheyanne standing in the wide doorway of the barn, her expression pensive. He felt for the girl. She'd gotten her boyfriend killed and her brother badly injured from her actions. Nothing he could say could change that.

She side-eyed him, chewing on her lower lip. For once, she didn't look outright hostile was a huge step in a new direction for them. "Grandpa said I should help."

"Sure, if you're feeling up to it?" Even though he'd prefer to work alone and was getting some relief from stretching his muscles and making them work hard, he also understood the girl needed to pick up the shattered pieces of her life. What better way than making a contribution?

"I'm fine. My stomach settled down. Laura thought it might be an attack of appendicitis, but it's all better now."

"Then grab a rake and start with one of the stalls that haven't been cleaned yet."

She wrinkled her nose but didn't complain. It was a start. For the next hour and a half, she followed his lead, working harder than he'd ever seen her before. Maybe there was hope for her after all.

They had finished the stalls and were heading to the

granary for fresh oats when Sam came racing across the yard, the look on his face making Connor stop in his tracks.

"What?"

"Jacob Evans, he needs our help. Right now! His family's under attack in Anchor. I just got word on the HAM radio."

"Shit." Connor dropped the handles of the feed wheelbarrow kept separate from the dung-filled one. "Where's Ben?"

"Last I saw him he was heading in to check on Hope."

The pair of them raced for the house, Wulver and Cheyanne hot on their heels. Ben opened the front door from the inside just as the four of them mounted the steps. He caught sight of them immediately. "What's up?"

"We need to take The Shark into Anchor. Jacob Evans, one of my employees, is in trouble. His family's being attacked."

"Is The Shark loaded and ready?" Connor asked. The intention was to keep weaponry inside the vehicle available at a moment's notice. Ben was in charge of seeing to it, but with Hope being so ill and every other thing that needed attention, he had to ask.

"Yes, saw to it this morning after we got back. Let's roll."

"I'm coming too." Faraday slammed the door behind herself as she hurried outside to greet them, her jacket still undone, boots untied, but an AK-47 at the ready in her hands.

"Cheyanne, you're in charge of telling everyone what's going on."

"I'm coming."

"Not going to happen. Stay here." Connor hated to see the step backward his words had done to their barely recovering relationship by the mutinous look that came over the teen's face, but he had no time for any pleasant formalities. It was do or die time.

The four of them raced for the shed where The Shark was housed. In less than a minute, Connor had started it up. Just as he drove it outside the building, Brady came bounding out of his new guest house. He raced across the yard before opening the side door of the vehicle. He was also loaded for bear holding on to an AK-47. He quickly strapped himself in not even bothering to ask any questions but nodded a greeting. Good man. He'd already shared he and his family were staying at Braveheart earlier this morning, even shaking hands on it. He'd tell the former lawman what few facts they knew on the way into town. Then he immediately headed them down the road toward the wall.

"We need to make sure no one is on the other side before we drive out," Connor said. Near the wall he braked and brought the huge vehicle to a full stop, its motor thrumming like a massive ship's engine hidden deep beneath powerful waves.

"I'll check." Sam jumped down from the passenger seat and hurried over to one of the viewing portals. He gave a thumbs up and unlocked the door. Soon as they drove through, he relocked the gate and climbed back into his seat.

Connor could feel the cold sweat easing down his spine. Already heated from the physical workout, now his heart was jackhammering in his chest with worry for the young family. The thought fired up every protective instinct in his body. Jacob and his wife Rachel had four small children and elderly parents living with them. To think someone was trying to harm the god-fearing

family was a crime of such magnitude it left him ready to blow the instigators straight to hell.

"Jacob told me yesterday they'd been plagued by an aggressive group from the trailer park. They've been scouring the neighborhood for food, demanding his friends and neighbors had over some of their stock. Everyone had given them a little at first, a few cans if they could spare it. They've been badgering people off and on for a few days, but today they came with weapons and wanted it all. And brought along a couple of assholes from the 666s gang as reinforcement." Sam said.

"Damn it. Why aren't people better prepared? Spending all their extra income on useless things like entertainment and recreation, fancy cabins at the lake. Taking expensive vacations. Drinking and using drugs, gambling it all away," Faraday said, her voice tight with anger.

"The real world was hard enough for many people *before* this all happened. They needed diversions just to get through the day. Can't blame them for that, girl. Now, stripped of it all, unable to even feed their families, reality has hit home with a vengeance," Ben said. "They're reverting to their natural state. Lost the slim veneer of civilization the last thousands of years had slowly managed to add to their lives in efforts to make them more humane to others. We had to learn empathy. Now it's all gone. We might as well get used to it."

No one said what Connor figured everyone was thinking. It was never going to be easy to get used to men acting like animals. It was creating a situation that was causing good men to have to do hard things. Things they could not have imagined a week ago.

A terse silence filled the interior of The Shark.

Connor kept his eyes fixated on the roadway, watching for any activity nearby. There was talk on the HAM radio of gangs of scavengers roaming the land, prepared to attack and take whatever they wanted. Of particular worry was the 666s, a gang of ruthless miscreants that began in Golden and had spread north, even before the current disaster descended on the state. Now they would be even more emboldened, knowing the law was hamstrung by too few police officers and too many of them. The bad men outnumbered the good these days like never before.

"What can you tell me about the layout of Jacob Evan's situation?" Brady asked.

"A bungalow on the west end of town, a new subdivision. Houses are packed in like sardines with small yards. He's located on the outer perimeter of a cul-de-sac. The back of his house faces a big open field. No coming up unseen. And easy pickings for a gang going door to door," Sam said, leaving Connor to concentrate on his driving. He was speeding, his entire body filled with apprehension to what they might find when they got there.

The miles were going by far too slowly, though he kept his foot pressed down flat on the gas pedal. They were burning fuel, but that was the least of their problems. Why hadn't Jacob brought his family straight back to Braveheart? He would have offered them sanctuary. The bunkhouse was huge, more than enough room for his extended family. He'd been away during a crucial time and now this was happening. A young family was in mortal danger. Yes, many families were now in danger. But it was a whole different thing when you knew them personally, not that his heart didn't bleed for all the other good men and women in a similar terrifying

predicament. Connor slammed the wheel in his frustration. No one said anything, but he felt their eyes on him.

Calm down. Going in hot is not going to help things. His father was suddenly there with him in the pilot's seat. A warm presence that brought a bittersweet feeling to flow through him. If only he really were here to offer his sage counsel though his wisdom over the years had not been forgotten. His dad had faced a few hostage situations during his tenure as a detective of the Anchor Police Department and then as chief of police. Some standoffs had ended well, no one hurt except maybe the perp who chose suicide by cop. But the 666s weren't worried about the law, they were a gang thinking they had the upper hand now. They'd be fighting them tooth and nail. What the hell were they going to find when they got there?

THIRTY-TWO
CONNOR

Day 8: Near Anchor, Alaska
   2:09 p.m.

Connor cranked the steering wheel of The Shark, easing past a group of vehicles half-blocking the road. Then he headed the massive vehicle down the sideroad that led into the cul-de-sac. The scenes his eyes had briefly lit on during the race from Braveheart to Anchor had burned into his retinas. Images of destroyed infrastructure, houses and businesses burned to the ground, unburied bodies lying in the ditch, horrors unimaginable only days ago. What the hell had happened in Anchor to bring it to the brink of destruction so quickly? This had to be gang related.

"What the fuck!" Sam said, his expression horrified at the devastation they were all witnessing in the stark light of the sun glinting off the thick glass of the windshield.

Connor's stomach lurched, firing off unease. It sluiced through him, halting his breath. They were too